I0716493

BLAKE

SAN FRANCISCO SHOCKWAVES
BOOK 5

SAMANTHA LIND

SAMANTHALIND.COM

Blake
San Francisco Shockwaves Book 5
Copyright 2023 Samantha Lind
All rights reserved.
Print ISBN 978-1-956970-18-0

No part of this publication may be reproduced, transmitted, downloaded, distributed, stored in or introduced into any information storage or retrieval system, in any form or by any means, whether electronic, photocopying, mechanical or otherwise, without express permission of the publisher, except by a reviewer who may quote brief passages for review purposes.
This book is a work of fiction. Names, characters, places, story lines and incidents are the product of the author's imagination or are used fictitiously. Any resemblances to actual persons, living or dead, events, locales or any events or occurrences are purely coincidental. Trademarked names appear throughout this novel. These names are used in an editorial fashion, with no intentional infringement of the trademark owner's trademark(s).
The following story contains adult language and sexual situations and is intended for adult readers.

Cover Design by *Jersey Girl Design*
Cover Image by Wander Aguilar
Cover Model : Zack Bradford
Editing by *Amy Briggs ~ Briggs Consulting LLC*
Proofreading by *Proof Before You Publish and Crystal Grizzard Burnette*

❀ Created with Vellum

CONTENTS

CHAPTER 1
BLAKE

I STAND AT THE RAILING, LOOKING DOWN ON THE expansive dance floor of the night club in Vegas with my brother, Justin, for his bachelor party. It's night one and we've got an entire weekend full of events before we return home for his wedding in a few weeks.

I take in the large number of people filling the floor below me. The DJ has the music cranked up loud and the crowd appears to be enjoying what he's laying down for them. I chuckle when I notice a few tipsy young girls stumble over to my brother and his group of friends, attempting to rub themselves all over the guys in their drunken state.

"Can I get you anything?" Barbie, the young server for our VIP section asks as she strides up to me. I'm sure the name is as fake as the breasts spilling out of her too-small top.

"I'm good for now. How are we doing on our minimum order?" I ask. I splurged and reserved the

VIP lounge for tonight and that comes with a minimum bar tab, which I figured wouldn't be hard to hit with a group of six of us.

"I can check again for you, but the last time I looked you only had a few hundred to go."

"I'm not that worried, thanks," I tell her before turning my attention back to the floor below.

A group of women join the dance floor and catch my eye. Their outfits give away the fact they are here for a bachelorette weekend, and it doesn't take long for guys to start surrounding them, handing over drinks as they start partying it up.

I take the last beer bottle from the bucket on one of our tables. I look around and catch Barbie's attention and point to the empty bucket, giving her a nod to go ahead and refill it for us before I head down to go let loose for a little bit.

I slip my way through the packed dance floor, finally making my way to where Justin is dancing.

"Finally came down off your throne to join us down here?" he jokes.

"Fuck off," I laugh before tipping the beer bottle back and drain it. "Want a shot or anything?" I ask as I shake my empty beer bottle at him.

"Tequila shots!" his best friend, Rodney, shouts from next to him.

"Tequila," Justin echoes, already a little drunk.

"All right," I agree and turn to push my way to the bar. I wait a few minutes before a bartender stops in front of me, but before I can get my order out, one of the women from the bachelorette party calls out her order from my side.

I turn to look at her, there's no way she missed that I was standing right here, waiting to order. "Maybe next time you'll be a little quicker," she said with a snicker.

"What can I get for you, sir?" the bartender asks, his lips tipped up in a smirk.

"Five shots of tequila and a bottle of water, plus the lady's tab," I tell him. "I've got a tab open with our table upstairs." I flash him the wrist band they gave all of us; each VIP section gets a different color so they can easily keep the tabs straight.

"Right away, sir," he says as he starts pouring all the shots.

"Where are you ladies from?" I ask the woman next to me.

"California," she answers.

"Who's getting married?"

"My best friend, Tess. Are you here with that rowdy bachelor party?" she asks as our drinks are pushed across the bar top to us.

"Yep, my brother is getting married in three weeks," I say as I scribble my name across the bottom of the charge receipt. "Thanks, man," I tell the bartender as I take the bottle of water from him and tuck it in my pants pocket so I can balance the five shot glasses in my hands.

I watch as the lady grabs the shots she ordered, doing the same with the balancing act. "If y'all want to come upstairs and join us, you're welcome to," I find myself offering.

"Thanks, I'll let the girls know." She flashes me a smile that has me stopping in my tracks as I watch as she slips away and into the crowd. I stay put until I see that she's reached her group, handing out the shots to each of the girls. They clink glasses, then knock them back. The way her throat bobs as the tangy liquid slides down has my body humming with a current I don't know how to explain.

I shake my head, trying my best to clear my thoughts, and start to move forward, pushing my way back to Justin and his buddies. I hand out the shots and watch as they all down them. "I invited the bachelorette group to join us upstairs," I tell him.

"Sweet, let's go party!" he calls out and starts to head off the dance floor.

When we reach the staircase, I let the bouncer that's parked there, making sure only those that have paid to be upstairs are the ones making it up, know that I've invited the group of girls to join us.

"No problem, sir," he confirms. "Do you want them to have charging privileges?"

"Sure," I agree. It isn't like I can't afford to pay for a few extra drinks tonight.

"Hi, I'm Tess. Thanks for letting us join you guys," the bride to be says as she enters our VIP section.

"The more, the merrier," Rodney tells her as he stands and tries to saunter over to the group of girls.

"I'm Blake. This is the groom, my brother, Justin.

That drunk asshole is Rodney, followed by Luke, Jimmy, and Brad." I say as I introduce all six of us.

"Nice to meet all of you," the bride says. "I'm Tess. This is my best friend, Raven." She tugs on the woman who I talked to at the bar, the one who is doing things to me without even trying. "This is Carrie, Morgan, and Kelsea." She rounds out naming the other women. If I had to guess, I'd say they are all in their mid-to-late twenties.

"How about a shot to kick off this party?" Justin suggests.

I flag Barbie down and we put in our shot order, along with some other drinks to chase the shots with. "I'll be right back with all of these. Did you want to put in any food or snack orders?" she offers.

"That probably wouldn't be a bad idea," I say. "Can we see that menu again?" I ask.

"Yep, I'll go grab one and be right back."

The girls have all started to mingle with the guys, that is except for Raven. She's standing next to me, silent as she watches our two groups as they commingle.

"Thank you again for inviting us. That was very kind of you. This place must have cost a fortune." Raven looks around the space, taking it all in.

"I offered to book it. I only plan on marrying off my brother once, so it was worth it." I shrug, not really caring what the cost was.

"Wow, you're paying for all of this?" she asks, her eyes bugging out of her pretty face.

I chuckle. "Yeah, let's just say my tax bracket is higher than everyone else's in the party." I don't like to flaunt my wealth but playing in the NHL for a handful of years, especially with my current contract, has set me up for a long ass time. I don't splurge often; I've tried to be smart with my money as I know my career could end at any moment with the wrong injury. I don't take my life for granted, ever.

"What part of California are you from?" I ask as Barbie hands me the menu to look at.

"Anaheim area, but I might be moving soon up to the San Francisco area."

"It's a great area, San Francisco that is," I tell her.

"You've spent some time there?" she asks.

"It's where my job is headquartered, so I spend a good amount of time there. That is, when I'm not on the road, and during my off time," I answer but try and keep it vague.

"There's an opening with my work up there and my brother got transferred there for his work earlier this year. It would be nice to be around family," she explains.

"Are you close with your brother?" I ask.

"Kind of. His work takes him all over North America. I usually only get to see him a few times a year, mostly in the summertime, but yeah, he's one of my best friends," she says, and I can tell by the smile on her lips that he means a lot to her.

"Sounds like my relationship with Justin. He still

lives back in our hometown, so I only get to see him and our parents a few times a year."

"Did you decide on anything?" Barbie interrupts to ask.

"Maybe a few of the grazing boards?" I say and show Raven the menu. "What do you think?" I ask her.

"The grazing boards sound good to me. The pretzel tower also sounds good."

"We'll do one of each grazing board and the pretzel tower," I tell Barbie. "Also, a bucket of waters, and go ahead and bring out two more buckets of the beers," I tell her as she enters everything into her little tablet. "Do you think the ladies would like a round of drinks? Maybe some cosmos or martinis?" I ask Raven.

"Oh, sure," she says. "Do you have raspberry mojitos?"

"We sure do," Barbie says.

"Then a round of those," Raven tells her.

"I've got the three grazing boards, a pretzel tower, two buckets of beers, one of waters, and five raspberry mojitos," Barbie confirms the order.

"Sounds good," I tell her.

"Are you two going to get over here and take your shots?" Tess calls out.

"I guess we're being summoned," Raven says to me as she places her fingertips on my forearm and pulls me over to be with everyone else. My skin zings with electricity at her touch.

I grab the shot glasses from the table and hand one to

Raven. "To tonight," I toast before clinking the glass to hers. "To tonight," she says before we both shoot the shot. The rum burns as it goes down, but I don't let it stop me from watching Raven as she takes her shot. Like when I watched her from across the room earlier, the way her throat moves when the alcohol slides down makes me think of the way her body would react to other things, mostly ones that happen while naked and underneath me.

CHAPTER 2
RAVEN

My head is a little fizzy thanks to all the drinks I've consumed tonight. I still can't believe that we're in this VIP suite with Blake and his group. They've been so friendly, not allowing us to pay for any of our drinks or food since we got up here. He said something about having to order a specific amount anyway to have the suite, so in reality we were helping them out in a way.

There is just something about him that has me constantly seeking him out. His easy personality and kind eyes are another level of sexiness. Not to mention his chiseled body. Even with clothes on, I can tell this man works out, probably to the extent my brother does. He's got that athlete style body, but maybe he's just one of those guys that likes to spend a few hours in the gym every day.

We get pulled into the group, everyone dancing together as the music picks up. Blake slides up behind me, his body pressing against my back, and there's no missing his hardness—everywhere. I shiver when his callused fingertips slide my hair off my shoulder. His lips are right next to my ear, and I'm sure he's noticed the goosebumps his closeness has caused. I can't control my body's reaction to him. "Is this okay?" he whispers.

"Yes," I tell him as I turn my head to the side so I can look back at him.

His hands fall to my hips as he pulls my ass harder against his groin. The one that is hard and pressing into my ass cheeks. I bring my hands up and hook them around the back of his neck, holding on as we bump and grind to the beat of the music. "Fuck, you're intoxicating," he growls into my ear after one of the songs ends.

"I could say the same thing about you," I tell him as I turn in his arms so we're facing one another. I can tell he wants to lower his head to mine and kiss me, but something is holding him back.

"Sorry to interrupt, but it's last call," Barbie, the waitress for our section announces. "Can I get y'all anything else before closing out the tab?"

I look around and there are still some unopened beers in the buckets on the table, as well as bottles of water.

"I'm good. Anyone else want anything ?" Blake says as he slowly lets me go but stops me from moving more than a few inches away from him.

I think we've all drank our limits as no one takes Barbie up on the offer to place one last order. "All right,

I'll get that check for you, Blake," she says before turning and walking out of the room.

"Are you sure we can't chip in on the bill?" Tess asks him as we wait for Barbie to return.

"I'm sure. I'd be paying for this room no matter what. Now you'll have extra money for the rest of your weekend, maybe treat yourselves to the spa," he says.

"We just might have to do that." She smiles at him. "Thank you."

"You're welcome."

Barbie returns and hands Blake a little black book. He opens it and scans over the slip before signing the slip and handing it back. "Thanks for your excellent service tonight," he tells her. I have to stop myself from acknowledging the fact I saw just how expensive this room was, or the fact that he tipped Barbie fifteen-hundred dollars tonight.

"My pleasure, and congratulations to both of you. I hope your wedding days are perfect," she says to Justin and Tess.

"Are you ladies staying close by? We can walk you back to your hotel," Rodney offers.

"We're at Caesars Palace," I say, "and thank you for the offer."

"That works out well, because we're also at Caesars," Blake says.

We all collect our things and make our way down the stairs and out of the club.

"Anyone want to stop at a craps table and try our

hand at some dice?" One of the guys, I think his name was Brad, asks as we start to walk through the casino.

"Sounds fun," Carrie says.

"Yeah, it does," Morgan adds.

"I'm in," Jimmy and Luke also agree.

"I think I'm going to head back to the room," I say. I'm exhausted and need to get some sleep before our full day tomorrow.

"Are you sure?" Tess asks.

"Yeah, I need some extra sleep. I'll be fine; stay out and have fun," I insist.

"I can walk her up to your room, make sure she makes it safe," Blake offers. The press of his hand against my back has my body humming, and not for sleep.

"Oh, you don't have to do that," I try to argue.

"I'll feel better if I know you made it back safe," he insists as he squeezes my hip.

"Okay, thanks," I give in. His touch has turned me to putty in his hands.

"Y'all have fun now, and don't do anything too crazy!" Tess calls out as Blake slips his hand around mine and leads me away from the noisy group.

We walk toward one the elevator towers, but I realize it isn't the one for where our rooms are. "Oh, this is the wrong tower for my room," I say as Blake reaches out to hit the button.

"I was hoping you wouldn't be ready to go back to your room quite yet," he says as he pulls me to stand in front of him. The elevator doors slide open. "Do you trust me?" he asks.

"Yes," I tell him. I don't know why I do, seeing as we just met mere hours ago, but something deep down tells me I can trust this man.

He escorts me onto the elevator and after tapping his room key against a keypad, he presses the penthouse button. My eyes go wide at that. Who the hell is this man?

"The penthouse?" I ask as I look up at him.

"Yeah. Like I said, I splurged this weekend." He smiles down at me as he tucks a strand of my hair behind my ear. "Can I kiss you?" he asks as his lips are already lowering to mine.

"Yes," I whisper just as our lips connect. The zap of electricity I feel just from the connection this kiss has made is like no other kiss I've ever experienced in my life, and that's saying something because I kissed a lot of guys in my first few years of college.

The elevator dings, pulling us out of the entrance we fell into as we deepened the kiss on our way up to the top floor.

We step off and Blake leads me down the hall to his door. He quickly opens it and leads me inside. The room is huge. The largest hotel room I've ever been in and seen with my own eyes. "Wow," I say as I take in the view. I walk over to the floor to ceiling windows, taking in the strip below us. I've never seen Vegas from this height, so it's definitely a new experience. "So pretty."

"Yes, you are," Blake says as he slips behind me. He moves my hair off my shoulder, exposing my neck before he starts to trail kisses along the exposed skin. I tilt my head slightly, giving him more access. The way his lips slide over my skin has my body on fire in anticipation of what else he might do to me.

I give him a few moments to kiss my neck before I turn to face him, pushing up on my toes so I can kiss his lips. His arms engulfing my torso as he picks me up so he doesn't have to bend down. I wrap my legs around his waist as he backs me up against the glass.

Our kiss is electric as we explore one another. Blake trails his lips from mine, back down my neck. "Fuck, I need more of you," he says into my skin.

I maneuver so I can grab the hem of my shirt and tug it up and over my head. My breasts are thrusted up, one, thanks to the push up bra I put on and two, because of the way he's holding me up.

"Fuck, you're perfect," he murmurs before lowering his head to my breasts. He covers the tops with sucking kisses, leaving little red splotches as he moves from one mound to the other. My bra pops open with one flick of his wrist, and the next thing I know, my bra is joining my shirt on the floor just as Blake pulls one nipple into his mouth, sucking hard as he does.

"Yes!" I cry out and arch my back to press my chest out further for his touch.

"So perfect," he says before taking my other nipple.

I grind my center against his hard cock as much as I can in this position. I need more, and he damn well knows it by the way he smiles against the skin of my breast.

"Tell me what you need, Raven," he instructs before circling my hard nipple with his tongue. "Do you need this tongue on your clit? Maybe deep in your pussy?"

His dirty words go straight to my center, making me even wetter for him that I already am. "Yes," I moan out, wanting all of that.

Blake steps back from the window and starts to move around the room, carrying me like it's nothing to for him to do so. We leave the living room and enter the bedroom. I take in the luxury of the room. The enormous king bed in the center is covered with what I'm sure is the best bedding they have in this hotel. More pillows than I've ever seen are also placed at the head of the bed. Blake deposits me on the end of the mattress, and I sink into its cloud like softness.

He steps back and starts to unbutton his shirt, quickly giving in and just tugging hard enough to cause a few of the buttons to go skittering across the floor. As he opens his shirt, I start to get a look at all the ink that covers his skin. He has a large piece that covers his chest, along with others on his arms. I reach out and trace around the large bird and skull. He watches me as I touch him, his muscles twitching under my fingertips, and I can't help but love the way his body reacts.

"Do you have a lot of tattoos?" I ask. He slips his shirt all the way off and I take in all the ink that covers his arms, mostly from the elbows up, as well as at least two on his lower torso. He's got one just above his pants and the other just the top of the letters peaks out.

"You could say that," he laughs. "Do you have any ink?"

"No, I'm not really a fan of needles."

"Ah," he says.

"I've always thought it would be neat to get one. I just don't know if I could handle the pain. I'm kind of a wimp, and then there's the needle thing."

"What would you get?" he asks.

"A stack of books or something to do with reading," I tell him. "I've saved so many book related ideas over the years, but just can't pull the trigger."

"What's your favorite genre?" he asks.

I suck my bottom lip into my mouth and chew on the edge of it before answering. I've had boyfriends in the past that thought my choice in books was ridiculous. "Romance, the sexier the better," I finally tell him.

"Oh, yeah?" He quirks a brow at me. "How sexy are we talking?" he asks.

"I don't shy away from the detailed books; I actually don't read much if it fades to black."

"What is fade to black?"

"When the book just alludes to the sex parts. Like they might kiss on page, but as soon as they enter the house or bedroom, the door closes and the scene fades to black, only for the story to start back again the next day or whatever. Kind of like how most TV shows and movies do things. I want the action. I want to know how he tossed her on the bed and ate her pussy until she came all over his face, or how he pinned her to the wall and slammed into her over and over again until he lost complete control and filled her with his cum."

"Fuck," he growls. "What else?" he asks, a spark of desire lighting behind his eyes.

I don't know where the boldness is coming from, but I stand up and decide to just show him. It's not like I'll see this man again ever in my life, so might as well take advantage of this one-night stand.

"How about I just show you?" I suggest as I unbutton his pants and reach in to grip his erection. His skin is hot and velvety to the touch. I drop to my knees and take his pants and boxer briefs with me. Blake steps out of his clothes and stands in front of me in all his naked glory. I take a second to take in his full body on display for me. The picture my mind came up with doesn't do him any justice with just how defined he actually is now that he's naked in front of me. I lean forward and swipe my tongue around the crown of his cock. I lick the bead of pre-cum that is leaking from his tip and am greeted with a sexy groan from his lips.

"God damn," he groans as I wrap my lips around his girth and slide as much of his length in that I can take before his tip hits the back of my throat. I breath through my nose, doing my best not to choke around his cock. I lick and suck as I feel him start to lose control. Blake gathers up my hair, holding it in his fist as I keep going, paying attention to what he likes the most. "All right, that's enough," he says as he pulls me off his cock. "I need your sexy ass naked and on the bed. Now," he instructs as he helps me stand up and strip my shorts and panties off.

I sit on the bed and push myself back, trying to maneuver as sexy as possible. My eyes never leave his body; they trail to his hard and shiny cock as his hand wraps around his length. He gives it a few slow strokes as he follows me onto the bed. I'm startled when he stops and stands up, leaving me all alone as he walks over to the dresser and pulls open one of the small top drawers. He pulls out a small box and brings it to the bed, then tears it open and pulls out the three silver packets before tossing them up by the pillows. "Now, where was I?" he asks before kneeling on the bed and crawling up until he's hovering over my body. "Fuck, you're so gorgeous."

"I'm already naked and underneath you. No need to impress me with your words."

"Fuck that. I'd tell you every day if you were mine to keep," he says before kissing me. His words hit me hard, *If I was his to keep.* Like who says things like that other than the heroes in the books I like to read.?

I get lost in the way he pleasures my body. The way his hands trail over every inch of skin, usually followed by his lips as if he's mapping my body to his memory. When he reaches my center, he positions himself between my thighs, tossing my legs over his shoulders. "You ready for orgasm number one?" he asks.

I can hardly think with his finger circling my clit already and the nearness of his mouth to my center. "I need your words, darlin'."

"Oh, shit," I moan at that southern drawl coming from his lips.

"What?" he asks, and I can tell he thinks something is wrong.

"Call me that again," I tell him.

"Darlin'." He quirks a brow.

"God damn, I didn't realize you were from the south. But that darlin' is dangerous. You'd better be careful using that on too many women."

Blake chuckles. "You can take the boy out of the south, but you can't take the south out of the boy." He shrugs. "But back to the question at hand. Are you ready for orgasm number one, darlin'?" He smirks when he says the pet name once again.

"Show me what you've got, Blake," I tell him, and that's all it takes before his tongue is replacing his fingers on my clit.

My body shakes as my orgasm builds and builds. My blood is boiling as his fingers slip inside finding my g-spot as he expertly works my clit over and over again. I slide my fingers into his hair, holding the back of his head to my center and buck my hips as much as a can as I ride his face searching for my release.

"Blake," I cry out the moment it hits me. My legs clench around his head before my body goes limp. My center pulses with the intensity of release.

I'm out of it, but I can feel as he kisses my inner thigh, then my belly, the underside of my breasts, a flick to my nipples as he slides up my body. He slips his tongue into my mouth, my orgasm on his tongue and lips. I normally don't like to kiss after oral, but I'm so caught up in the moment I don't push him away.

Once I've caught my breath and am more coherent, Blake reaches for one of the condoms and tears open the packet. I watch as he rolls it down his shaft. "Time for number two," he says before lining himself up and pushing inside my body. He stops once fully seated, allowing my body time to adjust to his size.

I lift my hips, encouraging him to start moving, and that he does. His thrusts start out slow and calculated, but the rhythm quickly picks up until we're both panting and chasing our respective orgasms.

"I need you there, darlin'," he grits out. I reach between our sweaty bodies and roll my fingers around my clit, giving it that little bit of pressure I need to crest over the edge for the second time tonight. "Fuck, squeeze that tight little pussy around my cock," he says as he thrusts through my orgasm, his spilling from him as he does.

CHAPTER 3
BLAKE

I wake up, the sun shining brightly through the windows. I roll over, expecting to find a warm body next to me, but I'm met with cold sheets.

I run a hand over my face, memories from last night clear as day in my mind. Which has me wondering why Raven ran. I sit up and check both sides of the bed, but don't find a note anywhere, so unless we run into each other again this weekend, I guess our night together is all we get.

My phone chimes from somewhere in the room, so I roll out of bed and go searching for it. It's still tucked into the back pocket of my pants from last night. I pull it out and see a few missed texts from Justin.

JUSTIN

You alive?

Did you run off and get married? We are in Vegas after all.

Seriously dude, where are you?

I can't help but laugh at his texts.

I'm alive, just woke up. I didn't get married, but I did have a good night, if you know what I mean. What's the plan today?

I take the phone with me into the bathroom and set it on the counter while I take a piss, then turn the shower on. As much as I hate to wash Raven from my body, I need to wash the sweaty booze smell from my skin.

We're all up and getting showered, then thought we'd go grab some breakfast before we head for the pool. I got confirmation we have a cabana for the day.

Perfect. I'm hopping in the shower now. I'll be ready in twenty minutes. I'll head to your suite when I'm done here.

Sounds good, bro.

I put my phone back on the counter and step into the shower. The hot water melts the tension in my muscles within seconds. I stand under the spray for a few minutes before grabbing my body wash and getting on with my day.

"How did the craps table treat all of you?" I ask the guys as we sit around the table, our breakfast orders just placed with the server.

"I won a few hundred by the end of the night," Luke says.

"I lost my ass," Jimmy grumbles.

"Broke even," Justin says.

"How was your night?" Brad asks, and from the smirk on his lips, I'm confident they all know Raven went back to my room with me.

"I don't kiss and tell, fuckers, but let's just say I didn't go to bed disappointed."

"Did she have any idea who you were?" Justin asks.

"I don't think so, or at least she didn't say anything if she did. Did anyone else from their group end up back in your rooms?" I ask.

"Nah, Raven was the only single one from the bunch." Luke says.

"What time did you end up walking her back?" Justin asks.

I must not hide the annoyance on my face well. "Oh, shit," Justin murmurs. "Did she slip out while you were sleeping?" he asks.

"Yeah, which I don't get. We had so much chemistry, but she was just gone when I woke up this morning."

"Something tells me she wasn't exactly looking for a one-night stand while in Vegas. Tess was kind of shocked she left with you," Justin tells me. "She said that she's usually the reserved and levelheaded one of their group. Something to do with her job as an attorney."

We never discussed what our actual jobs were, nor did we share last names, so I don't know why I'm so bothered by her slipping out sometime this morning.

"It is what it is, not like I have the time to dedicate to a relationship. Plus, I doubt she even lives near me, so it's a moot point," I tell the guys, but I think it's more for me than it is them.

Our food arrives shortly after that and we all dig in. I didn't realize I was so hungry until the plate of food was placed down in front of me. I ordered the steak and egg breakfast plate that came with hash browns, a side of pancakes and toast. I needed a good breakfast to soak up what is left of the alcohol from last night and to get a jumpstart on what we'll consume today.

SHOCKWAVES

THE PAST FEW HOURS HAVE BEEN MORE RELAXING THAN I could have asked for. The cabana at the pool was the way to go. We have servers checking on us all the time, keeping our food and drinks coming as requested. I called dibs on one of the loungers when we first arrived, and that is where I've stayed put the entire time. The other guys have been back and forth between here and the pool, but all I've wanted to do is snooze and people watch as I drink smoothies and feel sorry for myself. It's amazing how a woman slipping from my bed in the middle of the night can bruise the ego so much.

"Excuse me. I'm sorry to bother you, but are you Blake Watson?" a busty blonde asks from the opening of our cabana.

"Yes," I answer her.

"I thought so. I'm a huge fan," she says and tries to bat her eyelashes at me.

"Thanks," I say, trying to bite back my irritation at her bothering me in the middle of my time with friends.

"I'm sorry, ma'am, but this is a private area; you have to have a wrist band to be here," a security guard steps up to kick her out.

The blonde looks at me like I'm going to call off the big burly guy, but better luck next time, sweetheart.

"Asshole," she says, loud enough for both of us to hear before she storms off.

"Sorry about that, sir," the security guard turns to me and apologizes. "She slipped past while I was dealing with another issue. It won't happen again."

"Hey, no problem. She wasn't here long," I tell him. "I'm actually kind of surprised she knew who I was. I don't get noticed all that often unless I'm around a rink."

"Thanks for being understanding. Everything else going well?" the man asks.

"Got nothing to complain about," I tell him just as the guys all come back from the pool.

"Everything okay?" Justin asks as he takes in the security guard talking to me.

"Yep, just keeping security on their toes," I joke.

"Have a nice time," he says to all of us before returning to his post.

"What was that all about?" Justin asks me.

"Some chick recognized me and slipped past him. He kicked her out, and she wasn't too happy about it."

"Must be nice to be so popular," Jimmy jokes.

"Eh, I could take or leave the attention," I tell him honestly. Thankfully I'm not as well-known as actors or musicians are. I can at least live most of my life without being recognized by the average person, unless they are a hockey fan, and then I don't usually mind it. "Are you guys done with the pool, or what's the plan?" I ask.

"Yeah, we figured it was time to head back up to the rooms. Get showered and ready for dinner, then we'll see where the night takes us," Justin says.

We have reservations for dinner at one of the nice steakhouses but didn't plan anything specific for after that, knowing that Vegas has a lot to offer and to do on whim.

"Maybe we'll run into Tess and the rest of the girls again tonight," Brad says as we all collect our things.

My blood runs cold, thinking of seeing Raven again.

"I don't think we will. Morgan said they had tickets to one of the male stripper shows," Luke says.

"Male stripper shows?" I question and hope I don't give away my annoyance with that plan.

"Yeah, Chippendales or Thunder from Down Under.

I can't remember which one she said they were going to. They were just hoping to get Tess up on stage to embarrass the shit out of her."

The thought of Raven going to see a bunch of guys strip and dance for her has my blood boiling, not that I have any say in the matter.

We make our way back to the rooms. The guys are all splitting a two-bedroom suite, each room having two queen beds. I was the odd man out, so that's why I'm next door in my own. "Give me twenty or so minutes and I'll be over," I tell them as they continue down the hall to their door.

"Be ready to pre-game," Justin calls out. "I'm having the concierge set up some drinks before we head down to dinner." One of the perks of this floor is having twenty-four seven concierge service. They will bend over backward to make any request happen, which is nice considering how much I'm dropping on the rooms for this weekend.

"Aye aye, captain," I give him a three-finger salute before disappearing through my door.

Even though housekeeping has been in the room and cleaned up, I can still smell Raven as soon as the door closes. It might just be my mind playing tricks on me, but I swear she could be standing here in the room with me. All it took was one hit of the woman and I'm addicted and need another dose of her.

I press on, trying to shake her from my thoughts. I have memories to last me a while, even if I only bring them up when I'm alone in bed or the shower.

I pull out the shorts and polo I brought for tonight. Thankfully the restaurants we chose to go to here are a bit relaxed in the hot summer months with their dress codes. With my outfit picked out, I head to the shower to wash off the sweat from today, then get myself ready for another night on the town to celebrate Justin before his big day.

CHAPTER 4
RAVEN
ONE MONTH LATER

I stare at the two pregnancy tests resting on the counter. My eyes jump from the timer on my phone to the two tests. One is a digital. The other is a basic line test. The digital one has a flashing screen as it counts down to give me the results. Results I'm already ninety-nine percent certain will be life changing.

The timer on my phone startles me, even though I knew it was going to go off. I reach forward with shaky hands and turn off the loud song that is playing. *"You can do this,"* I tell myself before looking at the two tests.

Positive.

Both are glaring back at me. The digital has the word written out. The other has a plus symbol in the little circle. I can't believe my luck. Here I am, about to move, having just accepted a promotion at work, and about to become a single mother. I guess they were wrong with the saying, what happens in Vegas, stays in

Vegas. It looks like I've brought home a souvenir I never expected.

I clean up the trash from the two tests, tucking the positive tests back into one of the boxes. I'm not really sure what I should do with them, so I place them back under the skink for now. I've seen cute announcement videos and pictures, so maybe I'll use them for something like that once the shock wears off and I'm ready to start telling people.

My phone ringing startles me as I fumble to close the cabinet door and grab my phone from the counter without knocking it in the sink or off the edge.

"Hello," I practically croak after answering the phone.

"Hey girlie, what's wrong?" Tess asks. She can read me like a book she's read cover to cover a million times.

"Why do you think something is wrong?" I ask, trying to avoid answering her.

"Well, now, two reasons. One, you sound off, and two, because you just tried to answer me with a question. So, spill it woman."

I blow out a huge breath and tears sting my eyes. "I'm pregnant," I blurt out.

"Holy fucking shit. Did you just say what I think you said?" she screeches into the phone.

"My thoughts exactly," I deadpan.

"When, how, who's the father? Was it Blake from Vegas? Do you know how to reach him?" She rapid fire asks me questions.

"Blake is the only man it could be, even if we did

use condoms each time," I tell her, and my mind immediately jumps back to that night we spent together. I woke up in a panic and bolted without saying goodbye. I felt like a bitch for that stunt later, and then spent the rest of the weekend looking over my shoulder hoping we wouldn't run into him or his group of friends.

"Okay, so Blake is who we need to track down," she states like she's starting a to-do list for putting my life back together.

"Based on how long ago that was, I'd guess I'm six weeks along, but I guess I need to verify that with my doctor."

"I know this is all so shocking, but I'm happy for you. You're going to be the best mom ever," Tess says and fuck my hormones if her kind words don't make me cry.

"I have no idea what to do, Tess. I know his first name. That's it. I also know that he works part of the year in San Francisco, but that is it. I don't know what industry he's in, what his last name is. Nada. Nothing," I say as I collapse on the couch, the realization of my wild night coming back to bite me in the ass.

"Well, lucky for you, you have a kick ass best friend who will save the day," she says. "I'll be over in thirty minutes and will get to solving all your problems. What can I bring you to drink and eat, since I can't bring you wine?" she asks.

"I've been craving fruit smoothies the last couple of days. Can you bring me one?"

"Any flavor requests?" she asks.

"Strawberry banana," I tell her and my stomach growls at the thought of the yummy drink headed my way.

"Anything else?" she offers.

"No, I think I'm good. I'll see you soon," I tell her before we disconnect. I grab the box of tissues off the end table and attempt to blow my nose before stopping the tears from falling. I don't know how she's so confident she can solve all my problems, but if there is one person besides my brother I can trust with my life, it is Tess.

Like she promised, there is a knock at my door thirty minutes later. I peek out just to make sure it's her before I unlock the deadbolt and open the door.

"Why, hello, gorgeous," she says, giving me a once over before handing over the extra-large smoothie cup.

"I know I look like death. I haven't showered in two days. I've been sick and haven't felt like leaving my apartment. I'm sure I scared the DoorDash driver who had to bring me two pregnancy tests and a smoothie yesterday."

"You found out yesterday and didn't call me?" Tess asks, sounding offended.

"No . I actually ordered the tests yesterday but didn't have the courage to take them until today. I'd only known for maybe five minutes when you called. It was like you could sense that my life was changing in that moment."

"You know I would have brought you them and stuck around while you waited for the results."

"I know, but I was trying to stay in my denial bubble. What am I going to do?" I ask her as the tears return.

"Well, I think that once you get your butt up to San Francisco, I think you need to take a little trip over to Blake's house and just knock on his door, drop the news and see how he reacts."

"Small problem. I have no idea how to find him to even do that. It's not like I can take out an ad in the newspaper *'Missed connection—is your name Blake? Were you in Vegas one month ago for your brother Justin's bachelor party and spent the night with a woman named Raven? If so, call me at 555-123-9876. I have some important information I need to get to you.'* Like that would go over really well."

"I told you I've got you covered. I know Blake's last name. I know where he works and I'm pretty sure I could get you his home address," Tess tells me.

"How-why?" I stammer to ask.

"Justin and I friended each other on Facebook. I wanted to see his wedding pictures and hear all about his wedding after the big day. And since Blake is Justin's brother, I can tell you his last name is Watson. And an even crazier connection the two of you have is the fact that he's one of your brother's teammates." Tess drops the ultimate bombshell.

"What!" I exclaim, standing up to pace the living room. "He plays hockey? Professionally?" I can't believe this is happening.

"Yep, is the starting goalie for the Shockwaves." She sing-songs like she's the keeper of all knowledge.

"Camden is going to kill me, or him," I state.

"Why, it isn't like the two of you planned this or either of you knew who the other was. You are both consenting adults who had a wild night together and ended up with a souvenir from that chance encounter."

"Souvenir?" I quirk a brow at my best friend. "A baby is a little more than a souvenir."

"Duh, but you know what I mean. You aren't the first woman to get pregnant from a one-night stand and you definitely won't be the last. Just be thankful that I was able to solve the *who is he* issue so quickly. I can't believe I get to be an aunt in less than a year!" She cheers and I can't help but feel loved. Knowing that my child will be loved, even if Blake doesn't want to be in the picture, is a comforting feeling.

"I don't know how I'm going to tell him," I admit.

"Quit stressing about it. We'll come up with the perfect way to drop the news."

I chew on my fingernails, the stress of the situation overwhelming. "Okay, if you say so."

CHAPTER 5
BLAKE

I WALK INTO THE PRACTICE FACILITY. IT'S OUR FIRST DAY TO report for training camp, and I'm ready to get the season going. My time off was just what I needed. Time to relax, time with family, time to celebrate my brother getting married. There is still one night from this summer that plays like a memory reel in my mind on repeat. That night in Vegas I spent with Raven in my bed. It still pisses me off that she ran, but nothing I can do about it now except move on. Time to turn all my focus back to the game.

"Hey, man," Tristan, one of our veteran defensemen greets as he sees me coming down the hall. "Have a good summer?"

"Can't complain. How about you?" I ask as we slap hands and pull one another in for a man hug.

"Not bad. Just spent time with the family for the most part."

"Same. Got my brother all married off, otherwise it was just training and relaxing."

"Welcome back," our captain, Ryker, greets as he exits the locker room and joins Tristan and me.

"Thanks, Cap. How was the summer?"

"Busy. I forgot what it's like to have kids that aren't able to fend for themselves." He chuckles.

"Ah, can't say I can relate, but sounds like a busy one."

"Yeah, as bad as I feel about leaving Avery at home with the kids by herself, I'm kind of looking forward to nights on the road with a bed to myself and no crying babies."

"You'd better not let your wife hear you say that." Tristan laughs.

"No shit." Ryker laughs right along with him.

"You look like someone pissed in your breakfast," Tristan says to Camden Rowe as he makes his way into the hall. The Shockwaves acquired him in the off season. I don't know much about him, but I know he's been in the league for a couple of seasons.

"The fucker that knocked my sister up this summer. If I ever meet the piece of shit, I'm going to kill him," he seethes.

"Fuck, so what happened?" Ryker asks him.

"She had a one-night stand this summer and is now a few months pregnant."

"Damn, that sucks. Does she know who the guy is?" I ask.

"She says she thinks she knows who he is but hasn't

tried to contact him yet. She's trying to work up the courage to do it. Hell, it took her almost two months just to tell me and we talk all the time." He scrubs his face with his hands. "She just dumped the news on me while I was driving here, Said she wanted me to know before she arrives this week."

"Sounds messy," Tristan adds.

"If the guy doesn't know, maybe wait until he does before you go killing him. Give him the chance to step up to the plate and be a dad," I suggest.

Camden grumbles something incoherent but doesn't completely disapprove of my suggestion.

"I suppose we should quit our chit-chat and get ready for the team meeting," Ryker says as he checks the time on his watch.

We all push our way into the locker room, each of us going to our assigned spots and changing into the workout gear that has been set out for each of us. We get a lot of new team-issued clothing items during camp and the first few weeks of the season, all which we're expected to wear throughout the season.

"Welcome back, men," our head coach, Brett Jackson, calls out. "Be in the video room in five minutes," he instructs before leaving the locker room. Everyone busies themselves to be ready on time. Today is not the day to be late and piss Coach off.

I collapse into bed. My body is sore, but nothing I'm not used to after the first week of training camp. I give it my all, not because I'm worried about losing my starting job, but because that's just my work ethic. If I show up during practice, then I know Coach won't worry about me showing up when it really matters during a game. That's not to say that every athlete won't have an off game. I've had several over the years, but he knows the majority of the time he can count on me to pull my weight.

The jitters of games getting ready to start are rolling through my blood. We've had one pre-season game, but our rookie goalie, Charlie Stubbs, played that game. Coach usually starts pre-season with the rookies playing. Some are still fighting to make the final roster, while others he just wants to get those nerves out before the regular season starts.

SHOCKWAVES

Opening night has finally arrived. I went to morning skate, but only stayed on the ice for about a half hour, then spent another half hour on the bike before spending an hour being stretched out by the training staff. Being flexible is key to being a goalie, especially one that isn't constantly being hurt.

After that, it was back home to have lunch and take my pre-game nap. Now that I'm up from that and showered again, I button the vest of my three-piece suit and give my reflection one last look in the full-length mirror, happy with what I see, I grab my keys and phone and head for my garage.

I pull into the player lot at the stadium. While we don't have assigned spots, it is an unwritten rule where everyone parks. A pecking order so to say.

I give Damien, another one of our defensemen, a head nod as I see him get out of his car. He's an interesting teammate. Was always so broody and kept to himself. That is until last season when the team hired our social media manager and the two of them fell in love. She's brought him out of his shell, and he actually socializes with the guys.

"You ready for tonight?" I ask him as we both approach the employee entrance.

"Absolutely. Feeling really good about this season. I think we can make it far, if not all the way with this group of guys."

"I sure hope so," I tell him as we walk past the security guys, giving them a fist bump as we do so.

I stop in the dressing room to strip out of my suit and into workout clothes so I can go start my pre-game stretching routine. I stop in the trainer's room and grab a protein shake and go find a bike to start getting my legs warmed up on.

Camden sits down on the bike next to me, starting to peddle at my pace. "Hey, how's your sister doing?" I ask.

"She's settled into her new place here. Still hasn't confronted the douchebag who knocked her up."

"Give her time, I'm sure she's nervous. Especially if she doesn't really know the guy."

"I know she can handle it, but that doesn't change the fact I want to step in and do things for her. She's my baby sister and one of my best friends."

"I don't have a sister, so I can't say I'd know what I'd do in your shoes but think of it from the guy's perspective. What would you do if a girl you slept with once showed up weeks or months later to tell you she was pregnant? How would you handle that news?"

"I'd be scared shitless, but I'd step up. Probably ask for a paternity test, even if that makes me an asshole."

"See, so before you go making an ass of yourself, let him have a chance to step up to the plate and be a part of their lives. I'm not saying the guy needs to marry her, but he deserves the opportunity to be in the child's life and a father."

"I know you're right. Still doesn't curb the desire I have to pop the guy with a right hook once."

I don't hold back the bark of laughter at that. "I can give you that one," I joke.

We quit talking and turn to focus on our warmups, and after another five minutes on the bike, I head for the trainer's room again for my pre-game stretching routine.

My eyes slide up, checking the amount of time left on the power play. We're currently up one-nothing with just over two minutes left in the game, and we've got twenty-five seconds left on this power play. Even with the power play, I can't take my eyes off the play as all it takes is one timely placed poke check and a breakaway for the other team to get a scoring chance. Either that or the ultimate play where you get the puck to the guy coming out of the box just as his penalty expires and he's got a leg up on your defensemen, giving him a breakaway.

I bring my eyes back to the play at the other end. The guys are set up, passing the puck amongst three of them, looking for that open slot to shoot the puck at the goalie. Soapy tries, shooting it from the left circle, but it bounces off the goalie's pads and goes wide. Ryker scoops the puck up and sends it up to Damien who's at the top of the blue line. He keeps it in the zone and sends it flying off his stick and right over the goalie's shoulder. I raise my hands up in the air in celebration of the goal, then skate toward the bench to give my teammates a fist bump as they skate along the bench doing the same with everyone else.

"Hell of a goal," I yell at Damien as he passes by me.

"Fuck yes, it was," he yells back as I start to skate back to my crease.

We dominate the puck possession the remainder of the time on the clock, even when they pull their goalie and add an extra skater out on the ice. As soon as the final buzzer goes off, the guys jump over the boards, skating toward me for a huge team celebration, ending in a fist bump line amongst ourselves before we all leave the ice, our first win of the season under our belts.

I'm stopped by one of the game-day employees as I've been selected as the first star of the game, thanks to my shutout tonight. I'm handed a stick and sharpie, which I use to scribble out my signature on the blade of the stick. Jason Soaps is announced as the third star, followed by Damien as the second and then it's my turn.

"Your one-star player of the game, with an impressive shut out, stopping all thirty-one shots he faced, your goalie, Blake Watson," the announcer says, stretching out my name as he does so. I hit the ice, less my helmet, blocker and glove and skate across the ice where a guy is holding up his young kid who is hopeful to get the stick I have to give to one lucky fan. I toss it up and over the glass and into the kid's hands. The smile that fills his face is all I need to know that he's appreciative. I give the crowd a wave before I head back to the bench where the camera guys are waiting with a rink side reporter from the national broadcast team.

"Blake, walk us through how you were feeling and how you pulled off that impressive shutout tonight," Ashley says before turning the microphone my way.

"I've got a great group of guys in front of me this season. They did a good job of keeping control of the puck. Even when they lost control, they were always there to help me out. The first game of the season always comes with some new-season jitters, but I didn't notice that with anyone out on the ice tonight in a Shockwaves jersey."

"Thank you for your time. Go enjoy the celebration with your team," Ashley says before letting me go.

"Thanks," I say and smile into the camera before I do just that.

When I enter the locker room, the guys are all waiting for me, ready to spray me with water bottles as I walk in.

"Watson, Watson, Watson," they chant my last name as they pile on in celebration.

"All right! " Coach hollers out above the noise the guys are making. "Fucking amazing win tonight guys," he says as he looks around the room. "Watson, you proved why we have you between the pipes. Keep it up." I nod at Coach, knowing that I'd never let him down. "Enjoy the win tonight, but tomorrow we're back to practice and focusing on the next game. We've got a long road to the playoffs and we're just getting started," he reminds everyone.

As the newest team in the league, it feels like we have a target on our backs. No one believed we could form a winning team, at least not for the first few seasons, but we've proved them wrong and keep aiming to shock everyone by winning the ultimate prize at the end of the season by taking the cup.

I'm finally able to strip out of all my clothes and grab a shower. After Coach left, I was pulled for the media room, having to sit for ten or so minutes and answer all the questions thrown at me by different reporters. It isn't my favorite part of the job but a necessary one.

I slip my suit back on, forgoing the vest for my drive home. There are days I wish we didn't have to wear them after the game, but that's the way it is, at least for now.

"Night all," I call out to the guys still in the locker room when I'm ready to head out.

I sling my bag over my shoulder and push my way out of the door. There are a handful of people milling around, mostly family members of the players or staff.

"Hey, man," I stop to give James, a young man that came to hang out with the team last season after Damien met him and his mom a fist bump. "Did you enjoy tonight's game?"

"It was great. Nice shutout," he congratulates me.

"Thanks, couldn't have done it without the guys in front of me," I tell him. "Hi, Cassidy," I greet his mother. It's then I notice another woman standing down the hall. I think my eyes are playing tricks on me, but I swear it could be Raven.

"Hi, nice to see you again. Nice game tonight," she also tells me.

"How's your season going?" I ask James, turning my attention back to him.

"I made the travel team!" he tells me excitedly.

"That's awesome, man. Congratulations." I give him another fist bump. "You'll have to let Damien know when your games are. Maybe a few of us can come out to cheer you on."

"I think they might all die if a group of you showed up at their games," his mom says with a laugh.

"Maybe, depending on where the games are, perhaps we can sneak in the back," I tell her. My eyes flick back to the woman leaning against the wall. She's still looking down at her phone, so I only have a profile view from the corner of my eye.

"James, my man," Damien calls out as he exits the locker room and comes to a stop by my side. They exchange fist bumps like we did, and that's my chance to exit.

"Don't forget what I said," I tell him before I walk away.

I slowly walk down the hall, the closer I get, the more I know for a fact that the woman standing in the hall is Raven. I come to a stop a few feet from her and wait for her to look up at me.

"Blake." She gasps, her hand falling to her side. The look of utter shock or is that nervousness I detect.

"Raven," I let her name roll off my tongue. "How have you been?" I ask.

"Umm." She stammers as she looks around like she's checking for the nearest escape route. "I'm," she starts to talk, but we're interrupted by Camden.

"You ready to go?" he asks as he stops, positioning himself between the two of us.

"Yeah," Raven says, her eyes flicking between Camden and me.

"The two of you know each other?" I ask, motioning between them.

"I'd sure hope so," Camden laughs. "Blake, this is my baby sister, Raven. Raven, this is our starting goalie, Blake Watson."

Sister.

Pregnant sister.

The one that's pregnant after a one-night stand in early summer.

There's no way. *Right?*

"Raven," I start to say.

"You know?" she croaks out.

Camden stops, his head swiveling between the two of us as the pieces must click into place.

"You?" he seethes, and before I know it, his fist connects with my jaw.

CHAPTER 6
RAVEN

"Camden, stop!" I yell louder than necessary.

He shakes out his hand like he just hit a brick wall. I have to give it to Blake, He doesn't attempt to strike him back, but that could be the shock of being sucker punched out of nowhere.

"You're the fucker that knocked my sister up this summer?" he questions Blake.

Blake eyes fly to mine, questions burning in them.

"I hadn't told him yet," I speak up, tugging on Camden's arm as I try and diffuse the situation.

"Fucking perfect," Camden mutters under his breath but it's loud enough for all three of us to hear.

"Is everything okay out here?" an older man asks as he steps out to check on the commotion.

"Everything is fine, Coach," Blake says. "Just a misunderstanding," he tells him. I'm thankful he didn't throw Camden under the bus with their coach. That's all my brother needs is to be kicked off his team because I unknowingly got knocked up by one of his team-mates. What are the chances? There are what, like eight-billion people in this world, and I just happen to meet one of twenty-two other guys that make up the roster of a professional hockey team that my brother plays for.

"Then why am I hearing security saying punches are being thrown?" he barks.

"It won't happen again." Blake turns his full atten-tion to their coach. He must see the sincerity in Blake's answer that he lets things go, at least for now. I just hope that it doesn't cause problems tomorrow when I'm not here.

"Can we go somewhere to talk?" I ask as I bring the attention back to me.

"Of course. Do you want to come to my house?" Blake offers.

"Sure," I agree. "What's your address? I can meet you there."

He rattles it off and I add it to my phone.

"It's only a ten, fifteen-minute drive at most, espe-cially at this time of night," Blake says.

"Okay," I tell him before turning my attention to Camden. "I'll call you tomorrow." I can tell he wants to protest, but I used what he likes to call my court room voice, which he knows means not to argue with me. I've made up my mind and he's not going to change it.

"Fine," he agrees. "I'll be up late if you want to call before you go to bed," he adds.

"It's already late, I'll call you tomorrow," I reiterate before I lean in and kiss him on the cheek. "I love you, but you've got to let me handle this. I'm a big girl," I remind him.

I look at Blake and give him a wobbly smile. I knew this day was coming, I just didn't think it would be today or like this, but here we are and now it's go time.

Once out to my car, I pull up the directions to Blake's house on my GPS, which says I should be there in eleven minutes. I hit go on the directions and then tap the button to call Tess.

"Well, what happened to warrant a call at ten-thirty at night?" she says in leu of a proper greeting.

"He knows. It was dramatic, but at least he finally knows," I blurt.

"Holy shit. Okay, tell me everything," she says.

I give her the quick rundown of what just happened. I still don't quite believe it all as I'm recounting the last few minutes of my life.

"Damn, not how I pictured things going down, but okay. And you're on your way to his place now?"

"Yes, I should be there in about six minutes," I tell her as my eyes check the GPS.

"What is your gut feeling now that you know he knows?" she asks.

"I don't get the vibe that he'd be the kind of man to cut ties, but I guess only time will tell."

"From the little time I spent around him, he seemed to be a pretty stand-up guy, as did all the other guys in their group. I can't tell you how hard it's been to not message Justin," Tess confesses.

"You wouldn't!"

"Of course not, it wasn't my news to spill," she confirms.

"Okay, wish me luck. I'm pulling into his driveway. He's waiting at the entrance of his garage, so I need to go."

"Good luck. Maybe the two of you need to just bang it out. Get a few more orgasms out of the deal. It isn't like he can knock you up again." I can hear Tess cracking up on the other end of the line.

"Not helping," I whine.

"Go talk, hash it all out, make a plan, or don't tonight. You don't have to come out of this first conversation with all the answers."

"I know. Okay, got to go. He's staring me down." I tell her.

"Love you, call me tomorrow."

"Love you. Too, and will do," I tell her as I hit the end button on the call and then kill the engine. I grab my purse and push my door open. Once out of my car, I stand there next to the door, looking at Blake as he watches my every move.

"Shall we go inside?" he offers, motioning to the door inside.

I take a deep breath, then blow it out as I gather the strength to go get this conversation over with. I walk up and into his garage. Once I'm past him, he falls into step behind me as we make our way to the door. I step aside, giving him the room to open and go inside before me. He stops at a keypad and types in a code. The panel announces the security system has been turned off and is in standby mode.

"Would you like something to eat or drink?" he asks as we walk further into his house. It is huge, especially if he lives alone.

"Some water would be great, thanks," I tell him as he stops in the open living room. I can see into the enormous kitchen, and my mind starts picturing what it would be like to make dinner together in that space. What it would look like filled with baby items. I have to shake the images from my mind as I'm getting way ahead of myself right now.

"Have a seat, make yourself at home. I'm going to go change quick, if that's okay with you?" he asks as he hands me a glass of ice water. I accept it and set it down on one of the coasters on the coffee table.

"Of course. I'm not going anywhere, at least until after we talk that is," I say, correcting my statement. I cringe at how that first part sounded. I really hope he doesn't think I'm the clingy kind of woman who purposely put us in this situation, trying to trap the professional athlete.

I take a seat on the couch, sinking into the buttery soft leather. I take a few sips of my water, making sure my throat won't be dry once Blake returns and the talking starts.

"Sorry about that," he says when he returns, dressed in a T-shirt and some athletic shorts. The tattoos peeking out from the sleeves of his shirt bring back memories of tracing those lines that night.

"Nothing to be sorry about," I reply.

"So, when did you find out?" He jumps right in.

"About a month after Vegas, so mid-July."

"How far along does that put you now?" he asks.

"I'll be sixteen weeks tomorrow."

"Wow," he says and runs a hand through his hair.

"And before you ask, you are the only possible father, but I still understand if you'd like to verify with a DNA test."

"I-I," he starts to say something but stops before finishing, obviously wanting to think about what he's going to say next.

"I know this a lot to wrap your mind around, trust me, I've known for a while and am still getting used to things."

"Did you know who I was?" he asks.

"Not at all, but I also don't really keep up with athletes other than my brother."

He appears to like that answer.

"Why did you sneak out in the middle of the night?" he asks.

"I woke up and didn't want to risk you waking up to tell me that our night together was a mistake. It was one of the best nights of my life, and…well, now we have something to remember that night by."

"I'll be honest. I was pissed when I woke up and you were gone. I looked for you everywhere that weekend," he admits.

"I'm sorry. I should have handled that differently, but we can't change the past, we can only move forward."

"I take it you got the promotion with your job?" he asks.

"I did," I tell him, beaming with pride at that. "I'm now a junior partner and was moved here to San Francisco to take an open spot in the office."

"That's great. Congratulations."

"Thank you." I flash him another smile. We're sitting on opposite couches, the coffee table between us.

"How have you been feeling? Everything okay with you and the baby? You don't know what it is yet, do you?" He rapid fire asks me several questions.

I chuckle at his animated grilling. "I had a little bit of morning sickness the first few weeks, but as long as I ate little meals all day, I could keep it at bay. Thankfully that has subsided. I still get exhausted easily, but that's to be expected when you're growing another human. As for the baby, still too early to know if it's a girl or boy. We can find out closer to twenty weeks when they do the big scan, checking all the vital organs. Every appointment I've had so far has been picture perfect," I tell him. "Oh, would you like to see an ultrasound picture?"

"You have one?" He perks up at that, and I reach for my purse. I pull out the envelope I've kept in there since my first appointment when they did the scan to verify my dates and give me a due date.

"I do," I say as I go to hand it over, but instead of

taking it, he moves to sit next to me so we can look at it together. "This was back when I was only eight weeks pregnant," I explain, and point out the little bean of a baby at that time. "I've taken to referring to the baby as my little gumdrop," I tell him.

"Gumdrop; I like it." He smiles as he keeps looking at the picture.

"I want you to know I don't expect anything from you. You can be involved as much or as little as you want. I just ask that once this baby is here that you stick by your word. Show up when you say you will."

"Raven," he says my name, cutting off my rambling. "I'm not going anywhere. I will be there to take care of our child, and you," he says and my eyes flash to his. I can see something in his eyes. Desire, maybe?

"I don't expect a relationship out of this other than a co-parenting one," I say, my words coming out just above a whisper.

"Can I ask you something?" Blake asks.

"Of course," I tell him, but internally I'm freaking out what he might ask.

"Has that night, specifically our time together, left your mind for more than a few hours at a time?"

I can't answer him with words or else he might hear the crack in my voice, so I just nod.

"Raven," he says and shifts on the couch, angling his body to face me as best as he can. He cups my cheek, angling my face in his direction and tips it up so I have no choice but to look him in the eyes. "You haven't left my thoughts since that night. I wished I knew your last name and could have come searching for you, because I promise you, darlin'," he smirks after calling me that, and it does something to my insides. "If I knew more than just your first name, I would have tracked you down a long ass time ago. The connection we had isn't one I could ever describe to anyone else. Now that you're sitting here in front of me, in my house, I don't want to let you go. I want to explore where that connection can take us. Explore what it could turn into."

That was a ton to take in, especially in my emotional state. My hormones have been off the charts since getting pregnant. I've always been a pretty stoic person, but since this little gumdrop came along, I can cry at the snap of a finger.

"What are you saying?" I finally ask. My eyes are searching his as I wait for his answer.

"I'm saying I want a chance to see if we can be compatible together. We already know we are compatible in bed. Now let's see if that continues outside the bedroom."

I think over his words, kind of shocked he's taken the news so easily. I'm also shocked the connection we had that night seems to still be there. That pull that I felt that night is pulling me toward him. "I'd like that," I find myself saying.

I pull in a shaky breath but don't break the eye contact. I swear his head is slowly lowering to mine, and it is. I can feel his breath on my skin as he stops closing the distance when our lips are just a hair's breadth apart. My tongue peeks out to wet my lips, but the space separating us is so small, the tip of my tongue slides along his and that's all it takes for him to close the distance and slide his over mine.

I sink into his embrace, as the feel of his lips on mine takes me back to that night. What it felt to be worshiped by his expert touch. The way he played my body like he was an expert in making me feel the best I've ever felt.

I don't even realize I'm moving until I'm straddling his lap, my legs on either side of his hips as his hard cock presses against my very needy core. One thing I wasn't expecting with pregnancy is how horny it has made me. My vibrator can't keep up with how often I'm reaching for it.

"Fuck, I can't get enough of you," he says after pulling back for a full breath.

I sit back, my ass on his thighs, while one of his hands cups my neck and the other rests on one of my hips.

"Feeling's mutual," I say.

"Spend the night with me?" he asks.

I chew on my bottom lip, trying to decide if that's really a good idea.

"We don't have to have sex if that's what you're worried about," he says.

"What if I want to have sex?" I ask him.

"All I'm saying is I won't do anything you don't want or ask for."

"Take me to bed, Blake," I boldly tell him.

"Only under one condition," he says huskily.

I cock an eyebrow at him. "And what's that?"

"You don't try and slip out of my house before I'm awake in the morning."

"Okay," I promise him.

That's all he needed to hear before he stood up and started to carry me to his bedroom.

CHAPTER 7
BLAKE

I LEAN ON THE DOORWAY FROM THE EN SUITE BATHROOM TO the bedroom and take in my large bed in the center of the room. Raven is passed out after our three rounds of sex. I didn't think I could orgasm as hard as I did when we were in Vegas, but each time tonight it was just as intense as that night we spent together all those weeks ago.

I'm still wrapping my mind around the fact that she's pregnant with my child. I laid next to her for a while, my large hand splayed across the tiny bump that is starting to protrude. She said she hasn't felt the baby move yet, that usually comes in a few more weeks according to the book she read. I make a mental note to pick up a copy of the same one to read and catch up on, so I know what to expect.

I start to feel like a creeper, so I make my way back over to the bed and slide back in between the sheets.

Her warm body is like a beacon, pulling me into her orbit.

"Hmm," she hums into my chest as she settles against me. "You're so warm and comfortable, like home," she says sleepily. I don't think she's fully awake, but her words are soothing to hear, like they are the truth she can't say in the light of day quite yet.

SHOCKWAVES

I STAND AT THE STOVE, SCRAMBLING THE EGGS IN THE PAN as I sip on a cup of coffee. As much as I didn't want to get out of bed, I have to be at the rink in a little over an hour.

I hear rustling behind me, turning I find Raven walking toward me, one of my t-shirts hanging down to her knees. It engulfs her body, but she still looks sexy. "Morning, darlin'," I greet. "Can I get you anything? Coffee or juice?" I offer as she makes her way over to my side. She slips her arms around my torso, hugging me tightly.

I set my coffee down and wrap my free arm around her, holding her close. I drop a kiss to the top of her head and just relish this moment.

"It smells amazing in here. What are you making?" she asks as she looks up at me.

I can't help but smile down at her. She's makeup free, sex tousled hair, yet a peaceful look on her face. "I've got scrambled eggs almost done, bacon and hash browns are being kept warm in the oven, toast is ready to go down in the toaster and coffee is hot in the pot."

"Do you cook like this every morning?" she asks.

"Most mornings. I need a big breakfast to get me going on days that I'm on the ice. I burn a lot of calories."

"That makes sense," she says as she lets go and steps over to the coffee pot.

"Cups are in the cabinet just above the maker," I tell her as I turn the stove off and remove the eggs. I press down the toast, then pull the platter out of the oven with the hash browns and bacon. I start assembling my plate. "Do you want everything?" I ask.

"Yes, please. I'm starving, and this is all amazing."

I fix her a plate, just not as full as my own and take them to the table. Raven follows me, sitting down right next to me. We both dig right into the hot food, a comfortable silence falling between us as we do.

SHOCKWAVES

I WALK INTO THE PRACTICE FACILITY AND FIND COACH waiting outside his office, a stern look on his face. Just from his body language, I can tell he's pissed. *Fuck.*

"Coach," I greet, hoping his irritation isn't directed my way.

"Blake," he says my name and I know I'm not going to like whatever is going to come out of his mouth next. "I need you in my office," he states.

"Of course, sir," I say, no need to argue. I'm a man

and can deal with whatever fall out is coming after last night.

I enter Coach's office and find Camden already sitting in one of the chairs, as well as the team owner, Nathan, and our general manager, Philip Warner.

"Gentlemen," Coach starts, "we understand there was an incident last night between the two of you. I'd like to know the details of what happened and how we can move forward without any further issues. I'd hate to have to trade one of you to another team as we can't have a cancer in the locker room, especially this early in the season."

"I take full responsibility for the incident last night," Camden speaks up. "I let my emotions and frustrations on my sister's behalf get the better of me, and I can promise you that it won't ever happen again," he continues.

I look around the room at all the men filling this small office. As much as I don't want to divulge my sex life to essentially my three bosses, I've got to give them some details of what's going on and how those ties into Camden punching me last night.

"Unbeknownst to anyone, I met Camden's sister this summer while we were both on vacation in the same place. We parted ways without sharing contact information or last names. Thanks to her friend, she figured out who I was, but didn't divulge that information to Camden when she informed him she was unexpectedly pregnant." I pause talking, thinking over what else I want to say. "Camden wasn't very happy, thinking the man she'd met over the summer had left her high and dry while pregnant with his child. That man was me, but I had no idea about the baby until moments before he figured out the baby was mine and he punched me in the jaw."

"I should have kept my emotions in check. I take full responsibility for my actions last night and understand if there are consequences for them," Camden says, and I can tell from his body language that he's regretting the punch.

"We're all good, man," I tell him, reaching my hand across the space between our chairs for him to shake. He looks up at me, a look of complete shock filling his face. "I'd have had the same reaction if the roles were reversed," I assure him.

"I'm good as long as you do right by her and the baby." He accepts my hand, shaking it firmly.

"That won't be a problem."

I look from Coach, to Phillip, and to Nathan, giving them all a sincere look and nod. "I'm glad that we could get that cleared up," Phillip says.

"I expect last night's events to be in the past, and for there to be no issues moving forward. If something personal needs to be discussed between the two of you, I expect it to happen outside of these walls. Keep that out of my locker room," Coach says, and both Camden and I give him a nod of understanding.

"I give you my word that I've got no bad blood with Blake and can keep things as they were before my slip up," Camden assures everyone.

"If not, I'll just sucker punch him right back next time." I chuckle, trying to lighten the mood some. Thankfully my attempt doesn't fall flat, and I get everyone in the room to laugh with me.

"All right, let's get a move on our day. We've got some practice to get to," Coach says as he moves to open his office door and let us out.

"How was she last night?" Camden asks as we walk down the hall. "She never called me, so I'm sure she's pissed at me still."

"We had a good talk. I know that Raven and I haven't known each other that long, but we have a connection. One that I'd like to explore, especially now that our lives will forever be entwined. I give you my word I won't be walking away from her easily and never from my child," I tell him outside of the locker room.

"I appreciate that. You're a good man, Blake. I just can't believe the chances that the two of you met that weekend. Just goes to show how small this world is."

"It was definitely a shock," I agree with him.

Our conversation ends there, at that door. When we push into the locker room, the past is in the past and I have one hell of a future ahead of me.

I hop onto one of the bikes, warming up my legs before it's time to hit the ice. My body starts to relax as my muscles warm up. I'm like a well-oiled machine right now. My routine is down to science, all coming like second nature to me. "Everything good?" Ryker asks as he hops on the bike next to me.

"Yeah, all good today. How about you?" I ask him as I wipe my face with a towel.

"I heard Coach pulled you and Camden into his office first thing. What was that about?" he inquires.

"A misunderstanding. We're all good," I assure our captain. I know I could talk to Ryker. He's a good friend and teammate and would be a supportive person. I might just do that when we aren't here in this building. "Are you free to grab lunch after practice?" I ask.

"Yeah, shouldn't be a problem. We can talk more then," he agrees.

Practice takes my mind off things for the duration as we hone in on some plays Coach wanted us to work on. Things like the power play and penalty kill. Both are crucial to practice, so we are ready when they happen during the game.

I head straight for the locker room, quickly undressing so I can hit the showers. I don't want to keep Ryker waiting, and my stomach is already growling for some lunch.

I SLIDE INTO THE BOOTH, ACCEPTING THE MENU FROM THE young hostess that seated us. "Your server will be with you shortly," she says before stepping away from the table. Ryker sits across from me and looks over his own menu.

"Afternoon, gentlemen. Can I start the two of you

off with something to drink?" a guy, probably in his early twenties asks.

"Water is fine with me," Ryker tells him.

"Same for me," I answer.

"Do you guys need a minute or are you ready to order?"

I give Ryker a look asking if he's ready, and he gives me a slight nod. "I'll take the grilled salmon with rice, but is it possible to swap the asparagus for your green beans with bacon?" he asks.

"That's no problem," the server says "And for you sir?" he asks me.

"I'll take the shrimp fettuccini, and can I get extra shrimp on that?"

"Of course. It does have an upcharge for extra shrimp. Do you still want the extra?" he asks.

"Yes, please," I confirm.

"Anything else for the two of you?"

"I'm good," both Ryker and I say at the same time.

I wait for the server to turn and walk away before I drop all the details on Ryker's lap about last night.

"Holy shit," he says when I finish.

"You can say that again. I think I'm more shocked that Raven is Camden's sister than I am about the baby," I tell him.

"That kind of makes sense. So, what are your plans?" he asks.

"Bare minimum, we'll co-parent. I won't be a deadbeat father. I'll make sure I'm in my child's life and he or she has everything they could possibly need. If things work out between Raven and me, then that's just icing on the cake. We had an instant connection, and the moment I saw her last night, that pull to her was immediately back," I tell him.

"One small piece of advice. If you do end up with just a co-parent relationship, don't try to overcompensate for your time away due to the job with materialistic things. Kids are smarter than we give them credit for. I might have done that a time or two with Ellie when she was little, and it never worked out well in the end."

"Thanks for the advice," I tell him. "Any advice on how I take this connection from a one-night stand to something more without it seeming like I'm only doing so because of the baby?"

"My advice is start over. While you can't completely ignore the fact that the two of you are going to have a child in a few months, you can start with simple dates, build up that relationship. Get to know one another. If you both truly want it, it should come naturally. Don't make it all about the sex, not that I'm saying it isn't an important part of a healthy relationship, but it doesn't need to be the focus right now."

"I get it, and I think that's a smart idea. Taking it back to the basics." I ponder his advice as we both dig into our food that is delivered.

CHAPTER 8
RAVEN

I let the water cascade down my body, my muscles sore from my night with Blake . I still can't believe what has transpired in less than twenty-four hours. From breaking the news to Blake, to Camden punching him, followed by our talk and some incredible sex last night. My mind is all over the place. Could you consider that make-up sex?

I still don't know what to think about Blake and me. Did we have chemistry? Yes, yes, we did. So much chemistry. The way that man made my body tingle and pulled every last drop of pleasure out of me is like none other, but I also can't wrap my mind around how we go from that lust to something more, especially now that we have a child to think about. The baby has to be our priority.

The water starts to cool slightly, so I quickly wash my hair and finish my shower. Once out, I lather every inch of my body with lotion before getting dressed. My belly has just slightly started to pop out. Most days I can still fit in my looser fitting things. I know sooner than later I'll need to take a trip to a maternity store, but for now, loose dresses it is.

Thankfully, I still have a few days off before I return to work. With my move, I took some much-needed time off. Thanks to movers, all my stuff was delivered, and the furniture all assembled and placed where I wanted it to go, so all I've had to do is unpack and put every-thing away. With all of that done within a couple of days, I've had the rest of my time to fill my fridge, start to learn the layout of my area, and figure out my route to work and other places I'll be going to on a regular basis.

After breakfast, Blake and I talk a little bit, and I agree to come back over to his place for dinner and for us to talk more. We really need to talk and figure things out before falling into bed again. As good as the sex is, we can't let it take precedence to the issues at hand.

Once I'm dressed, I pull out my laptop to check my emails and make sure all my address change updates have gone through for all my bills.

I have no idea how long I get lost in taking care of things, but I'm pulled out of my stupor when my phone rings. I glance at the phone and see Tess's goofy face filling my screen.

"Hello," I greet and can hear the cheerfulness in my own voice.

"Well hello to you too. Based on that chipper voice,

I'm going to guess things went really well last night with the hockey hottie."

"You could say that." I smile and remember just how good it felt to finally tell him the news and get a feel for where he stands on being in the baby's life. I also can't forget how good it felt when his tongue was on— I shake my head making that memory flee while I'm talking to my best friend.

"Did you get any talking done or was it just a fuck fest?" She laughs into the phone.

"We talked..." I trail off. "Some," I add for good measure.

"Got it. Glad to know the chemistry is just as strong as it was in Vegas. So, when are you seeing Mr. Hot Stuff next?" she asks.

"I'm going back later today so we can talk more and have dinner."

"Are we talking with words or grunts and moans?" she snickers.

"Oh, shut up." I crack up laughing. "There will be lots of words. I think I'm going to tell him I'm willing to see where this leads, but we need to start over. Go on some dates and make sure we vibe before falling back into bed together."

"I want to hear all about it later," she says. "Well, all except the sex details if you end up not being able to keep your hands off one another. All I care about is that he takes care of you and knows how to make it good for you, so if that means dialing it back a few notches and starting over, then do just that. Get to know one another outside of the bedroom. My advice is if the dick isn't good, then don't settle."

"That won't be an issue." I smile as my mind wanders back to his tongue on specific body parts. I have to shift my thighs as my center starts to ache for him. "Changing the subject now. When are you coming to visit me and see my new place?" I ask.

"Does next weekend work? Jeremy is going to a race with some of the guys, so I was thinking it would be the perfect time to come see you."

"Next weekend is perfect," I tell her and am excited that I'll get to see my best friend so soon.

"I'll book my ticket and send you the details!"

"Sounds like a plan."

We talk for a little longer before she's got to go. Once off the phone, I check the fridge and pantry and start making my list of the things I've forgotten to get already. I want things in order when I return to work on Monday, so that only gives me a few days to do just that.

SHOCKWAVES

I PULL INTO BLAKE'S DRIVEWAY AND FIND HIM WAITING FOR me in the open garage door. He's standing there in all his tall sexiness with his tattoos on display thanks to the fact he's only got on shorts and sandals. I'm sure if you looked up sexy man in the dictionary, you'd find his picture right next to it along with the definition.

I park and get out of my car. We both close the

distance between each other like we're somehow pulled together by a magnetic force. "Hello, darlin'," he drawls, and I swear he brings out that very subtle accent just for me. "How was your day?" he asks as he tips my chin up to look at him. His other hand rests on my hip and holds me close.

"Good. Took care of some emails, change of addresses, things like that," I tell him. "How was your day? Was my brother on better behavior today?" I wince waiting for his answer.

"He was, and we're all good," he assures me.

I smile up at him after hearing that and am rewarded with the sexiest smile just before Blake presses his lips to mine in a searing kiss. "Let's go inside. We don't need to give my neighbors a free show." He squeezes my hip before sliding his hand to my lower back where he keeps it as we walk inside his house.

"Can I ask you something?" I ask as we walk into the living room.

"Anything," he confirms.

"Why do you live in such a big house when it is just you?"

"For a few reasons," he says as we both take a seat on one of the couches. Today we sit together, rather than across from one another like we started out last night. "When I was picked up by the Shockwaves in the expansion draft, I knew I'd be here for a while. I had some long conversations with the owner, Nathan, and our GM, Phillip. They knew my desire to be with one team for multiple seasons. I knew I had the skill and ability to land the starting position, and they had faith in me to not disappoint them. It's why they agreed to the fifteen-team no-trade clause as part of my contract. With that stability in my contract, I was willing to buy a house rather than just rent a place like some guys do. Another reason is I like my privacy when I'm home. Living in a condo only gives you so much of that. A house, especially one in a subdivision like this, comes with some privacy that you can't get elsewhere. I also wanted a home that I could comfortably entertain in, host my family when they come to town, and maybe one day fill with a family of my own," he says sincerely.

"That all makes perfect sense. Does your family come out often?" I ask.

"My parents usually make it out at least twice every season. They also try and make the games in Nashville and Dallas since those places are the closest to my hometown."

"Which is where exactly?"

"The outskirts of Memphis," he says. "Where are you from? I know you just moved here from Anaheim, but something tells me that isn't where you are from originally."

"I'm from Minneapolis. Moved to California for college, stuck around for law school and the rest is history," I tell him.

"Do you go back to Tennessee in the summer?" I ask.

"I usually make it back for at least a few weeks, but I

don't own a house there or anything. I just stay with my parents when I go home. This is the only house I own. I tend to spend time either in Minnesota or Canada for some training during the summer. I also don't mind coming back here early and just relaxing until it's time to report back to the rink."

"Sounds like Camden. He's always all over the place during the off season," I say and start to laugh.

"What's so funny?" Blake asks.

"Just thinking back to when we met in Vegas. I don't know if you purposely were vague about your job, but I think it's funny how we were both trying to describe the same job when it comes to you and Camden."

"Now that you say that it is kind of ironic and funny." Blake chuckles.

"Speaking of my brother, I know you said outside that things were all good, but are you sure?" I press.

"Yeah, Coach called us both into his office. The owner and GM were both in there, but Camden took full responsibility for what happened last night. It's all water under the bridge. I gave the higher ups a vague rundown of what transpired and how last night's events culminated, and they were understanding to a point. Just wanted to make sure it wasn't going to cause issues going forward and we both agreed it wouldn't. No other disciplinary actions for either of us came of it."

"Oh, good. I was worried. I haven't talked to him yet, so I hadn't heard what happened today."

"I think you should call him; he was worried about you," Blake tells me.

I nibble on my lip as I think about what I'm going to say to my brother. "I know, and I will, but not while I'm here."

"What if I was to invite him over for dinner?" Blake asks.

"Do you want to do that?" I ask.

"Darlin'," he says, and I swear he knows that melts my panties by the way his eyes smolder. "There is no bad blood between Camden and me. We're good, I promise. And there's no better time than now for us to get closer. No matter what happens between us romantically, our lives will be tied together for life thanks to the baby growing inside you."

"Do you do that on purpose?" I find myself asking.

"Do what?" He gives me a questioning look, but he's also smirking, so I know damn well he knows what calling me darlin' does to me.

"Call me darlin'."

"Should I call you something else?" He quirks a brow.

"Darlin' works just fine," I admit.

"That's what I thought." He leans in and kisses me tenderly.

"What are you doing to me?" I ask when we break apart. I suck in air like I haven't had a full breath all day.

"I could ask the same of you," he says before kissing me again. This time he maneuvers my entire body until it is under his, splayed out on the couch where we make out like teenagers left alone for the night. When we break apart, I push against his chest, making him sit up and I follow. "What's wrong?" he asks, his brows pulling in as he looks me over.

"As much as I enjoy kissing you, I think we need to back up a bit. Really get to know one another and see if this is something we both really want to pursue."

Blake sits back and rubs a hand over his face, then up and through his hair. "I had the same thought earlier but also can't stop this desire to kiss you."

"I guess it will take some effort on both of our parts to avoid it for a while," I state.

Blake quirks a brow. "How long is a while?" He breaks out into a huge grin.

I smack his chest playfully. "I don't know, but let's just see how things go, okay?"

"Okay," he agrees.

CHAPTER 9
BLAKE

"WHAT CAN I HELP WITH?" RAVEN ASKS AS I FLIP THE pork chops on the grill. After our little talk about tapping the breaks and starting over, I texted Camden and invited him over for dinner. I wanted to prove to Raven that things were good between her brother and me.

"How much time is left on the timer for the pasta?" I ask.

"Ten minutes," she says.

"You can get the salad mixed up, maybe bring out some plates, and we can have dinner outside."

She heads back inside, and I look over at Camden. He's nursing a beer as he watches the two of us from where he sits at the patio table. "If I didn't know better, I'd think the two of you were an old married couple," he says.

"Like I told you before, there's this strange connection between the two of us. On one hand, it feels like we've known each other forever, but on the other, we know very little." I tell him. "We just fit, like we were made for one another, but we did decide to take things slow, get to know one another as friends, maybe go on a few dates before we make any further decisions on where we take things between us."

"Okay, you can stop with all the sappy shit." He chuckles into his beer bottle. "But I think taking things slow is a good idea."

"Sorry, man, but I won't stop talking about her, even if she is your sister."

"Just keep the bedroom details to yourself." He shudders as he says that.

"I don't kiss and tell." I chuckle at his discomfort.

"Good, keep it that way," he says just as Raven comes walking out with a large salad bowl on top of a stack of plates. Camden jumps up and takes them from her, helping to set things down on the table.

"What are we keeping what way?" Raven asks.

"Bedroom details," he shudders again. "I don't need that shit being talked about in the locker room."

"Don't worry, darlin'," I wrap an arm around her waist and tug her into me, "I don't share those kinds of details with anyone, especially not my teammates." I give her hip a squeeze instead of the chaste kiss I want to drop on her lips, reminding myself to keep things friendly.

Raven smiles up at me before she slips from my arms and heads back inside to gather the silverware and the pasta dish from the oven, making separate trips to deliver both to the table. I pull the pork chops off the grill just about then, and we're ready to dig into our dinner.

We sit around outside, talking and getting to know one another better. Raven and Camden both start telling me stories from their childhood. I liked seeing the sibling bond the two of them have, as it gave me a little window into their relationship.

"Got any good embarrassing stories to share with me?" I ask Camden.

"Don't you dare," Raven leans forward, shooting first her brother a death glare before she turns it on me. Little does she know what that look does to me below the belt.

Camden chuckles before taking a swig of his beer. "Oh, do I ever." He smirks at his sister before turning his eyes my way. "There was this one time at a football game," he starts to say and Raven groans and flops back in her seat.

"Really?" she cries out, "You have to start with that one?"

"It was homecoming, so the stands were completely packed. It was also a chilly night, so the cheerleaders all had on their track suits to keep them warm." Camden continues and I watch Raven as he continues to tell me this story. "Before the national anthem, they were doing their normal routine getting everyone pumped up and ready for kickoff. As one of the tumblers, she set up in the end zone, and would do a routine of flips all the way to the center field. With about three flips left, somehow her pants caught on something and as she flipped, she pulled them right off her body. Flashed the entire stadium her behind, but more impressively, she finished her routine like nothing had happened."

"It was so embarrassing," Raven added. "I didn't have on my cheer covers, so it was my actual under-wear everyone saw. Had I had on our regular uniform, I wouldn't have been so embarrassed."

"I can see how that'd be embarrassing. Did anyone give you grief about it?" I ask.

"Eh, a few people teased me about it, but it quickly forgotten once the next big drama dropped."

"You've heard one of my embarrassing moments, so tell us one about you," Raven says.

I think for a few moments, trying to decide what memory I should share with her. "When I first got called up to play in the AHL, it was a few months into the season, so the guys on the team already had good bonds. They were a great group and filled with guys who loved playing pranks on each other. When I was led into the players area that first day at the practice facility there was this statute, or let me rephrase that, what I thought was a statue until it jumped out at me and scared the shit out of me. The coffee I had in my hand went flying and ended up all over the place. They got my reaction on film and everything." I chuckle remembering the day like it was yesterday. "It wasn't just for my benefit. One of the guys was playing a prank on the entire team as they arrived, and I just so happened to show up on that day."

"Oh, shit." Camden laughs.

"Yeah, it was a great way to be welcomed to the team."

"How is that embarrassing?" Raven asks.

"I screamed like a little schoolgirl. They loved playing that video back whenever they had the chance," I state.

"I still think my story was worse."

"I won't argue with you there. I have another one and this did happen in front of a rink full of spectators." I smile at her across the table. "Same season as my previous story, I was called up for a game to the NHL. The guys played a prank on me before I left. They covered my blades with clear tape. I don't know how I missed it, but when I went to hit the ice for warmups, I completely biffed it because of the tape covering the blades."

"That sounds dangerous," Raven says, and I can hear the concern in her tone.

"Eh, we've all done it. Probably wasn't the smartest thing to do going into a game, but they had no idea I wouldn't make it for morning skate and have it happen then."

We continue to exchange stories for another hour or so. I can tell Raven is getting tired. I'm sure growing a baby will do that to a woman.

"It looks like you need to get yourself home and off to bed." I finally say to Raven after she tries to hide another yawn behind her hand.

"I should," she agrees, but I also notice a hesitation on her part.

"Are you okay to drive home?" I ask. While we'd agreed to take things back to friends, that doesn't mean I can't still take care of her in a platonic way.

"I'll be fine," she says, yawning again. "I'll chug some water and be good to get home. I promise," she insists.

I gather the last few things from the table as we all make our way inside. The kitchen clean up can wait until I have Raven safely in her car and on her way home.

I watch as she gathers her purse, phone, and water bottle that she topped off before we head for the door.

"Thanks for dinner. I'm glad we could clear the air tonight," Camden says as he offers up his fist for a bump. I tap my knuckles against his.

"Aww, aren't you two so cute," Raven teases the two of us. "Such a bromance."

"Better than the alternative," Camden snickers. "I could be decking him again for knocking you up."

"You do and I'll castrate you myself," Raven warns him. Just the word *castrate* has the blood draining from my own balls as they try and crawl back up inside my body.

"Now, now, bodily harm isn't necessary," I warn. "From anyone." I look into Raven's eyes, then quickly to Camden's before returning to Raven's.

"There goes all my fun," she huffs, then breaks out into

a fit of giggles. I pull her into my arms, wishing once again I could kiss the breath right from her lungs. I settle for a tight hug. She wraps her arms around my torso, leaning into our embrace. The small swell of her belly presses into my abdomen and it takes every last drop of self-control to not reach down and rest my hand on the swell of our child.

"Let me walk you out," I finally offer. Raven tips her head back so she can look up at me.

"Thanks again for tonight." She smiles at me, and the look on her face is complete contentment.

I tuck a loose strand of hair behind her ear before I drop my hand back to her shoulder. I stop myself from running my fingers down her cheek or from dropping my lips to hers. I settle by pressing a quick kiss to her forehead. Friends could kiss each other on the forehead, right?

I step back and reach for the door, opening it so everyone can exit. "I'll catch you tomorrow," Camden says as he throws up a hand, waving it quickly as he walks to his car, leaving Raven and me in his dust. "Call me tomorrow, sis," he says to Raven.

"Will do. Love you," she calls after him.

"Love you, too," he tells her before sliding into his car and quickly backing out.

I walk Raven to her car and open the door. "Thanks for coming over. Do you have plans Sunday afternoon?" I ask.

"I don't. What did you have in mind?"

"I'll pick you up at twelve-thirty. When do I need to have you home by?" I ask.

"Um, by nine or so. I go back to work on Monday morning, so I need to get to bed at a decent time."

"Okay, I'll make sure you're home by then," I assure.

"Do I get any hints as to what we'll be doing or where we're going?" she asks.

"Nope, just dress comfortably," I answer.

"Okay, it's a date." She smiles at me.

"Our first one." I wink.

"Good night, Blake," she says before sliding into the driver seat. I wait for her to be settled before shutting her door, then rap my knuckles on the roof twice before stepping back so she can reverse down my driveway. I watch as she does, raising a hand to wave as she stops to put the car in drive after reaching the end and turning out. She gives me a quick little wave and smile, then disappears down the road. My heart does this little flippy thing that I'm coming to associate it doing, but only with Raven.

CHAPTER 10
RAVEN

CAMDEN

The ticket for you is at will-call. There should be a family pass with it so you can come down after the game if you feel like sticking around for a little bit.

Thanks for that, excited to come watch you again tonight.

Me or your baby daddy?

Can I be excited to watch both of you? {smirking emoji}

{eye roll emoji} I see how it is. You find yourself a hockey player and now your bother is just chopped liver who provides you with tickets. I see where I fall on your list.

Oh, shut up. You know I love you. At least you're on the same team and I don't have to cheer for your rival.

I'd disown you!

No, you wouldn't. You don't have it in you to hate me for any reason.

Okay, you might be right. Love you, sis. I've got to lay down for my game day nap.

Have a good one. I'll see you tonight. Kick some ass tonight.

CAMDEN GIVES MY LAST MESSAGE THE THUMBS UP reaction but doesn't text anything else back. I place my phone into my purse and grab my keys. I need to go do a little retail therapy. I know it won't be long before I need some business clothes that can accommodate my bump, so while I have the time, I head for the mall to check out what maternity clothes options I have.

I bum around the mall, not finding a top that I love. I picked up one dress, a pair of slacks and a blouse that will work for in-office days. I might have to start some online shopping for court-appropriate attire, but with no cases currently on the docket, I don't have to worry about that for a little while longer.

I grab a smoothie from the food court because they are still one of my favorite cravings, before I head for my car and then back home. I put my new purchases away then pull out my jersey for tonight's game. I change into a pair of jeans and Shockwaves T-shirt Camden gave me. It hugs my bump, showing it off. I stare at my reflection in the mirror, taking in the changes that my body has gone through in the last sixteen weeks. I rub a hand down over my belly. *"Mommy loves you, Gumdrop."* I'm still wrapping my mind around the fact that I'll have a real live baby in about six months.

I arrive at the arena before warmups start. I've always enjoyed watching my brother play hockey. It was always his happy place. No matter what else was happening in his life, hockey was there for him. The friendship—or family, as he describes it—he has made with all the different guys he played with along with their families. He still keeps in touch with the billet families he lived with while playing junior level hockey. It was strange to have him so far away those few years, but I knew he was chasing his dream of playing professionally, and I loved the fact he was making his dreams come true.

I pick up my ticket and pass from the will-call window and check to see where he got me a seat for tonight's game. When I came to the last game, I was in the lower bowl, almost on the blue line. I don't usually care where I'm sitting, just as long as I can watch him play. I stop at one of the concession stands and grab some food and a bottle of water, then head for my seat. I laugh when I find my section – behind the goal, where Blake happens to be in net currently as the guys all shoot at him. I make my way down, finding my seat right on the glass. What a jokester my brother is sometimes. I'm sure he did this on purpose, but I'm going to take this as his approval for whatever is to come between Blake and me.

I take my seat and dig into my chicken strip basket, paying no attention to the warmups on the ice. "Um, ma'am," the guy next to me says.

"Yeah?" I ask around a mouth full of chicken.

"I think one of the players wants your attention."

I look from the guy to the glass, where my brother is standing and tapping on it. He gives me a shit eating grin before mouthing "Like your seat?"

I give him an eye roll, but follow it up with a thumbs up, which just causes him to laugh hard enough his head falls back. He presses his closed fist against the glass, and just like we've done since he was playing as an eight-year-old, I tap my own fist against the glass as if we're fist bumping.

"Do you know him?" the man next to me asks once Camden skates away.

"Since the day I was born," I tell him. "He's my brother."

"Awesome, he's a great player. I'm glad we picked him up this off season."

"Yeah, I'm glad he's here, too. I missed being able to watch him play in person," I find myself telling the man.

My attention is pulled back to the ice when the goalies swap who's in net for the next few minutes. Blake stops at the glass, standing right where Camden just stood. He smiles at me when our eyes connect, and the butterflies I get every time we're near one another take flight. He winks, then skates away, stopping near the center ice line where he drops down and stretches out. It appears he's talking to one of the goalies on the other team who is also stretching out. I've seen goalies do this often, and it makes sense that they'd have friends who play the same position as they do on other teams. My eyes follow Blake as he continues through his warmups with the team.

As Blake leaves the crease and the seconds tick down to the end of warmups, he circles around the back of the net and taps the tip of his stick blade on the glass as he passes by. I smile at the attention, but don't say anything so I don't draw attention my way more than I already have.

"You friends with Watson?" the guy next to me asks.

"Yeah," I answer nonchalantly. "I've met most of the team thanks to my brother."

"That's so fucking cool," he says.

I shrug, because while it is cool, they are still just a bunch of normal guys. They just so happen to get paid a shit ton of money to skate around on sharp little blades, chasing a puck and knocking into one another as they attempt to get the puck in the back of their opponent's net. "I know most fans don't think this, but they are all really just normal guys." I've never understood why people put athletes on pedestals, but I guess I should be thankful for my brother's sake as the money those fans spend on tickets and merchandise help pay his salary.

I sit back and finish my food while the Zamboni is

mopping the ice in preparation for the first period when a woman comes and sits in the open seat next to me. I take in her appearance and immediately get the vibe that she's here for the eye candy of the players and not because she's a fan of the game. "Excuse me, but did I hear right that your brother is on the team?"

"Uh, yeah," I answer, not really wanting to give this woman any information.

"That's so cool," she says all bubbly as she twists a lock of hair like women do when flirting with someone. "Do you think you could sneak me down to the locker room after the game?"

"Sorry, that's not allowed. Only players and staff can give out passes for the family area, and I didn't even get one for tonight's game." I lie and am thankful I put my pass in my purse and not around my neck like I some-times do.

She huffs, obviously not liking my answer. "Oh, come on, I highly doubt they'd turn you away if you showed up at the entrance."

"Even if they wouldn't turn *me* away, I wouldn't bring someone I've never met with me to 'sneak' them in," I tell her using air quotes. "I'm not about to risk my credentials for a stranger. Sorry, not sorry."

"You don't have to be such a bitch about it," she sneers before a security guard taps her on the shoulder. "What?" she yells as she turns to face the person tapping her.

"Time to go. You can't be bothering the other

patrons. We've already gone over this. Don't make me kick you out and press trespassing charges."

"Fine," she huffs and stands up out of the empty seat next to me. I watch slack jawed as she stomps up the steps, the security guard never leaving her side as they both head up.

"That chick is crazy," the man next to me says.

"I gathered that," I tell him.

"She's been kicked out so many times for being obnoxious. Likes to wear inappropriate clothes and press herself up against the glass, trying to get the guys' attention during warmups. I guess her attempts at bagging one of the players isn't going all that well."

"I can't imagine why," I say as we both laugh at her expense. "I don't usually like the term puck bunny, but damn if she doesn't fit the definition to a T."

"I wish they'd just trespass her, so we don't have to deal with her almost every game."

"Are you a season ticket holder?" I ask.

"Yep, bought them as soon as they went on sale after the expansion team was announced. I grew up playing youth hockey. Still play in a beer league, but mostly, I just love watching the game," he tells me.

"That's so cool. As you can imagine, hockey was a huge part of my life growing up."

I chat with the guys next to me until the lights go down, signaling the intro is about to start.

The game is full of excitement. The Shockwaves strike first on a power play only three minutes into the first period. Dallas answers back just a few minutes later when one of their wingers sends a puck flying at Blake and somehow finds the smallest hole above his shoulder and buries the puck in the back of the net.

The rest of the game is back and forth. We score, they score. We take back the lead, they tie it back up. I'm on the edge of my seat for the last few minutes of the third period, hoping like crazy that we can keep our current one-goal lead.

"You've got this, Blake," I whisper under my breath over and over again, cheering loud along with everyone else in this building when he makes save after save.

My eyes flick to the game clock, where I see twenty seconds are left. That's all that he has to make it through before this game is in the books. Dallas has pulled their goalie, giving them the extra attacker, but also leaving their net empty. The puck slides along the blue line between Dallas players. They are obviously looking for an opening, but Blake is zoned in and stops the puck. He flicks it up to clear it out and everyone in this arena watches as the puck goes up, then comes down around center ice, where it goes rolling on the ice, and is headed straight for the empty net at the other end. The players all race down that way, but before they reach it, the puck trickles over the line. The goal horn blasts as the entire building erupts in the loudest noise I've ever heard in my life. The final buzzer also rings out, but I don't think anyone is even paying attention to that as the guys on the ice all skate back to pile onto Blake as they celebrate his goalie goal. They aren't all that common, but definitely a cool thing to witness.

The refs review the video playback to verify the puck crossed the goal line before the time ran out, and they confirm that with one-tenth of a second left, the puck crossed and was a good goal. I have tears in my eyes as they all celebrate the goal and win yet again after the confirmation by the ref.

CHAPTER 11
BLAKE

THE EXCITEMENT FROM SCORING TONIGHT IS STILL PUMPING through my body. I wasn't even trying to score. I just wanted to clear the puck out of the zone and give my teammates a break as the final seconds ticked off the clock.

As I enter the locker room, I'm greeted with chants as they all spray me with water bottles as I walk in. This is the second time they've done this to me this season, which is a bit much, but I've been on fire so far. "Watson," they chant as I soak in all the excitement.

"Hell of a game, boys," I tell them as I hold up a hand for them to quiet down.

"I don't think I have to elaborate much with who tonight's game puck goes to," Coach announces, and everyone quiets down. He hands me the game puck, then hands me another puck that has white hockey tape wrapped around it and is marked with the date and time of my goal, as well as the words *1st NHL Goal Puck – Blake Watson.*

I accept both, then pose for the social media crew waiting in the locker room to capture all of this tonight. I've seen my teammates pose with pucks like this for their goal achievements, but never thought I'd be doing the same during my career. I think every goalie dreams of scoring a goal before they retire, and my name joins the short list of goalies who accomplished this one feat in their career.

I finally can strip from my gear, then grab my shower bag and make my way to the much-needed shower. While I'm soaping up, images of Raven behind me, pounding on the glass as she cheered for us fill my mind. If I'm not careful, images of her will lead to a situation I don't need happening below the belt while I'm in the locker room showers with my teammates around. I push those thoughts of her out of my mind and finish up.

With a towel wrapped around my waist, I head back for my stall. I towel off, then pull on a clean pair of boxer briefs. I toss the wet towel into the dirty laundry bin, then step into my trousers. Next comes my undershirt, and finally I finish the ensemble with a button down. I button the shirt up, then tuck it into my slacks. I fasten them up, then buckle my belt and call it good.

"Did Raven stick around?" I ask Camden as I grab my bag and close it up.

"Not sure. I gave her a family pass, but she wasn't

sure this afternoon if she'd be up to sticking around or not. Said she'd play it by ear."

"Gotcha," I say. "I guess I'll find out shortly." I fist bump my teammates that are still here as I exit, accepting additional words of affirmations about my goal.

I finally make it out of the locker room and down the hall. I don't notice her at first, but then I find her like my eyes are drawn directly to where she's sitting down on a chair against the wall. One of the security guards must have gotten her one from an office as they don't usually have any out here.

"Everything okay?" I ask as I crouch down so I'm at her level.

Raven's eyes pop open and then I realize she'd nodded off as she waited for one of us to come out.

"Yeah." She yawns. "You had an amazing game. What a goal there, mister." She reaches out to place her hand on mine, and it wasn't until the moment our hands connected, I grasped just how much I missed her touch.

"That was pretty impressive, huh."

"It was the best goal I've ever seen, and that's saying something."

"I didn't miss the way you pounded on the glass behind me," I say, a full-on smile pulling at my lips knowing that she was cheering me on tonight. I kind of like the idea of her right behind me.

"That was a new view, not that I'm complaining." She winks. "Although it was kind of strange, especially when people around me realized I had a connection to the team."

"Oh, was everything okay?" I ask, concerned for her safety.

"The guys next to me were cool. After Camden came and talked to me for a few seconds during warmups, I told them he was my brother because they asked if I knew him. Then when you came to the glass, I just said we were friends. No need to share our history with complete strangers." She stops talking to suck in a breath.

"Makes sense, seeing as that's no one's business but ours," I assure her.

"I know." She gives me a quick smile. "Then this crazy chick sat down on my other side. She must have overheard me tell the guys Camden was my brother. She was brazen enough to ask if I'd sneak her down here after the game, then got pissy when I told her no. I lied and said I didn't even have a pass for tonight, so she was SOL. Security ended up coming down and escorting her up the steps. The guys said that she's often down there causing a ruckus, trying to get anyone on the team's attention."

"I know exactly who you are talking about. She's a pest that just won't go away. We have a hard and fast rule in the locker room that no one is to bring that crazy chick into our inner circle."

"Dang, that's good to know."

"Yeah, not someone we want to get her claws into one of the guys. She's bat shit crazy, and we just don't have time for that during the season. Enough about the crazy lady. We should get you out of here and home into bed. Are you good to drive home?" I ask, ready to swoop in and save the day if needed.

"I'll be fine. I need to get up early tomorrow so I can get my grocery shopping done before you pick me up for our date."

"Let me walk you out then," I offer as I stand to my full height, then offer her a hand. Raven slips hers into mine and I wrap my fingers around her small hand.

"Leaving without saying goodbye?" Camden asks as he comes jogging up to the two of us.

"I was falling asleep waiting on you," she tells him as he pulls her into a hug. Raven drops my hand so she can hug her brother, then slips it right back into my hand once they are done.

"I'm just giving you shit," he says as the three of us start walking to the exit.

"Where are you parked?" I ask Raven.

"The parking garage across the street."

"I can either walk you over, or drive you over, your choice," I tell her.

"You don't have to. I can walk," Raven tries to argue.

"Not happening, especially at this time of night. So once again, do you want me to walk you over or drive you over?"

She worries her bottom lip between her teeth as she thinks over my offer. "I guess drive to keep you from having to walk back, and I am a bit tired."

I escort her out to the players parking lot and directly to my car. I open the passenger door, letting her sit on the butter soft leather of the sports car. "This is so nice. Not car seat friendly, but definitely nice."

"Don't worry, darlin', I've got a car seat friendly SUV in the garage already."

I watch as she shudders from me calling her darlin'. I know it might be mean, but I love seeing what that does to her, so I have no plans of stopping any time soon.

Once she's settled, I shut the door, then deposit my bag in the back seat and round the driver's side, sliding behind the wheel. I fire up the engine and it purrs to life. "It even sounds sexy," Raven hums.

"You like that, huh?" I tease as I back out of my spot.

"Yeah, I do."

"Noted." I smirk and tuck that nugget of knowledge away for safe keeping.

I exit the players' parking lot and easily make it down the street and into the parking garage across from the stadium. Since it is well after the game ended, the traffic is all gone, and only a few cars remain in the structure. "What level did you park on?" I ask as the lift gate opens, allowing me to drive all the way in.

"The second level, over by the cross bridge." I head up the ramp and easily spot her car parked where she said it would be as it is the only one left in the area. I pull up next to it, put my car in park and quickly get out so I can open her door. "Thank you," she says as I offer her my hand so she can stand.

"Of course. You sure you'll be okay getting home? Want me to follow you?" I offer.

"I'll be fine. I can text you when I make it home, how's that?"

"I guess I'll settle for a text." I pull Raven into a hug. Her arms easily wrap around my body, and I swear she melts into my body. My heart does this fast beat thing when she's in my arms, but that is as far as I can take it right now. *We're taking it slow*; I remind myself—at least for now.

"Congratulations again on the goal. I'm glad I was there to experience it."

"Thank you. I'll see you tomorrow at twelve-thirty."

"See you then," she agrees, but she doesn't pull from my embrace. We stand there in that parking garage, holding one another for a few minutes.

"As much as I don't want to let go of you, I know you are tired and need to get home. So, either get back in my passenger seat and come home with me or get your fine little ass in your car and drive home."

"I know," she huffs and reluctantly steps out of our embrace. Her car beeps as she touches the handle, unlocking the doors. I hold it open while she slides behind the wheel and buckles the belt.

"Night, darlin'." I lean in and press a kiss to the corner of her mouth. "Sweet dreams," I say before stepping back and closing her door. I take a few more steps back until I can lean on my own car and watch as she starts up hers. She gives me a little wave with her fingers as she puts the car into reverse and backs out of the parking spot and heads down the ramp. I quickly round my car, getting back behind the wheel. I slam it into reverse as I buckle myself in and speed down the ramp, not wanting to lose sight of her car.

I'm in luck since there is hardly anyone left out on these streets, so I easily spot her car a block down. I pull out of the garage and head in her direction, all the way to the interstate, where I follow her on, even if it is the opposite direction than my own house. I have this deep need to protect her and our unborn child, so if that means following her home so I know she made it safely, then call me a stalker because I'm doing it.

My phone rings over the car's speakers a few minutes later and I start chuckling as I hit the button on my steering wheel to accept the call.

"You aren't very good at hiding the fact that you're following me," Raven says.

"What gave you the impression I was trying to hide?" I ask, and thankfully I can hear the playfulness in her voice.

"You've got me there," she laughs.

"I just had this need to see with my own eyes that you made it home safe."

I can hear her blow out a big breath. "Where did you come from?" she asks.

"Tennessee, ma'am." I know it is a smart-ass reply, but what else am I supposed to say.

"You're going to make it hard for me to resist you, aren't you?"

"Damn straight. Why fight it darlin'? We've got chemistry in spades, so why not explore it?"

"I never said we couldn't explore it. I just thought taking sex out of the equation for a little while would allow us to get to know each other as friends and then if we still felt that way, we could go back to exploring that part of our relationship. I just don't want either of us to feel pressured because of the baby."

"Don't overthink it, darlin'. Things will come naturally if they're meant to be."

"Shit," she says, and I'm instantly on alert.

"What's wrong? The baby okay?" I ask as panic sets in.

Raven starts laughing harder, and my blood pressure lowers slightly as I wait for an answer. "That was my exit. I was so caught up in talking to you I wasn't paying attention to what exit we were at."

"You scared me, woman," I tell her as we both move over to the right lane for the next exit.

"Sorry about that, not my intention." She's still giggling as we turn at the light.

We stay quiet as we make the next few turns, then pull into her condo building's parking lot. Raven pulls up to a large garage door and waits as it lifts. I like knowing she lives in a secure building and has dedicated parking.

"Are you good, or do you want me to stay?" I ask since we're still connected on the call.

"I'm good. Text me when you get home."

"Okay, shouldn't be too long," I tell her before we disconnect the call.

The parking lot has another entrance, so I just pull through and exit from there, quickly make my way back to the interstate and back in the direction of my house. I push the speed limit, wanting to make it home so I can text her. I don't want Raven to stay up waiting on me, and I know she's already exhausted, so I have to assume she'll get ready for bed as soon as she gets up to her condo.

CHAPTER 12
RAVEN

BLAKE

Made it home. Are you in bed?

Just about to slide between the sheets. Had to wash my face and do my nightly routine.

What does your nightly routine look like?

You really want to know?

I wouldn't ask if I wasn't interested. I want to know everything about you.

It's pretty basic and boring. Wash face, brush teeth, apply nightly moisturizer, then pj's and into bed. Before I fall asleep, I put in my retainer and then usually fall asleep reading.

Simple is good.

> Were you worried I was one of those women who had a 20-step process.

Not really, I didn't get those kinds of vibes from you.

> Not to cut this cute little conversation off, but I can hardly keep my eyes open. I'll see you tomorrow.

Dream of me. {winky face}

SINCE IT IS MY LAST DAY BEFORE RETURNING TO WORK, I didn't set an alarm. I knew I would wake up in plenty of time to get ready for my date with Blake. One of the most noticeable changes, other than the obvious physical ones, is the increased need to pee in the morning. I glance at the clock, and I am surprised to see I made it until eight. I'm usually up between six-thirty and seven most mornings.

I stand and stretch, feeling the twinges in my muscles as they stretch to accommodate this baby. I make my way to the bathroom and take care of business, then hop into the shower to get my day started.

Blake told me to dress comfortably, so I pull out a cute sundress . It's supposed to be sunny and in the low seventies today. I pull my hair half up, getting it out of my face for the day. I decided after pulling it up to add some curls to help give it some volume since this is a date after all. I move on to a minimal amount of makeup with some mascara and small amount of blush. I don't like wearing a full face unless I absolutely have to, so this is what it is going to be for the day.

Once done in the bathroom, I head for my bedroom where I lather my skin with lotion before pulling on some bike shorts, so my thighs don't rub together under my dress. The last thing I need today is a rash from walking around. I add the last cute bra that still fits, which reminds me I need to go bra shopping soon. These girls are getting a little out of hand all ready. I'm a little scared how much larger they are going to get when this baby is born, and my milk comes in. Once my dress is on, I give myself a once over in the mirror and can't believe just how big my belly looks today. I swear it grew overnight. Either that, or this dress is more form fitting than I remember. Either way, I think I look cute, so I'm sticking with it.

With my morning routine done, I grab a small breakfast and start working on my lunch and dinner menu for the week. I like to plan ahead each week; it helps keep me from eating out too often, while also not wasting the food I do buy. I will often meal prep one weekend a month. Rather than do it weekly where I'm left to eat the same thing every day, I'll make up multiple dishes, then freeze them in single serving containers that I can just pull out from the freezer to defrost and heat up. It works well when I'm only cooking for one all the time.

Since I haven't done that since moving here, I'm going to have to improvise until I can get my freezer stocked up with easy meals. I check what I already have and make a plan around that, then fill in my list with what I need to pick up to make it through the week.

By the time I finish with that, it is already eleven-forty-five, which means Blake will be here in less than an hour. I take the time to submit my grocery order for delivery for tomorrow night after work. I love that feature and know it will come in handy once the baby is here and I'm alone and don't feel like taking them out shopping.

My phone ringing makes me jump, glancing down at it I see Tess's face on the screen. I tap the green circle, accepting her incoming FaceTime call.

"Holy hot momma!" She whistles as she takes me in.

"Look at how much my belly has popped!" I say, propping the phone up and stepping back so she can see me better.

"Damn girl, that baby *has* popped. I can't wait to rub your belly when I see you next weekend! What's got you all dressed up on a Sunday?"

"Blake is picking me up in about a half-hour for a date." I tell her and know I'm blushing based on the heat coming from my cheeks.

"Aww, how is Mr. Sexy Pants?" she bounces her brows at me as she asks.

I can't but help but laugh at her expression. "He's good. I went to the game last night and he scored a goal! It was so awesome to see."

"Wait, I thought he was supposed to stop the puck?" she asks, confused.

"He is, but he got a goalie goal. The other team

pulled their goalie so they could have an extra player to try and tie up the game in the last minute or so. He stopped the puck and cleared it up and over everyone. It had so much power behind it that it slid all the way down and into the other net!"

"Holy shit!" she exclaims. "That must have been exciting. I'll have to look up a video of it."

"I'm sure it's all over the internet. Goalie goals aren't that common."

"So, where are the two of you headed on this day date?"

"No idea. He wouldn't tell me. Just told me to dress comfortably and that he'd be here at twelve-thirty."

"So mysterious. You'll have to call me later and tell me all about it."

"I will, I promise. It was so cute. When he asked me out and I agreed, he asked me what time he had to have me home by, so I think he's planning on something all day. I told him my curfew was nine since I have to go back to work tomorrow."

"Are you excited for that?" she asks.

"Yes, I'm ready to get settled into my new office. I stopped in the other day just to check in and see my office. It's so charming! Maybe you can help me decorate it next weekend!"

"Of course! We can go shopping for all the pretty decorations. I'm so damn proud of you. Working your ass off to move up the ladder, rolling with life's changes like a pro, and maybe just maybe finding yourself a fine ass man who I think will treat you like the queen you are."

"You know how to make a girl feel good," I tease my best friend.

"Don't you forget it. I'm serious. You deserve the entire world, and I have a good feeling about where things are headed for you."

"I love you. The only thing I hate about taking this promotion is moving away from you."

"Maybe I'll convince Jeremy to move up to San Francisco," she muses.

"That would be the best gift ever. Tell him I'd owe him for the rest of my life if he moved you here."

"I'll work on him," she says, and I notice she winks, so he must be in the room with her.

"Hi, Jeremy! If you bring my best friend to me, I'll love you forever!" I sing-song loud enough for him to hear.

"I'll take that under advisement," he chuckles as he comes into the camera view. "You're looking good there, momma," he compliments.

"Thanks. Starting to feel like I won't ever stop growing."

"I can't say I understand, but pregnancy looks good on you. You're glowing."

"Tess, you'd better go jump your husband. He's got me all emotional."

"Yes, listen to Raven," Jeremy teases his wife as he kisses her neck.

"Give me five minutes and then I'm all yours," Tess says to Jeremy.

"I'm holding you to that," he tells her as he taps at his watch.

"I guess I'm on the clock." Tess laughs. "I'll be waiting for your call tonight to tell me all about today and tonight. Maybe we'll both get lucky today." She smirks.

"Only you, I'm afraid. One date isn't long enough to get to know one another without sex complicating things," I remind her but feel like I'm just reminding myself.

"If you say so. Okay, I've got to go. My husband is being demanding. Love you."

"Have fun, you two. Love you, too."

Our FaceTime ends and I can't help but smile about our conversation. I love Tess and Jeremy together. They really are one another's soul mate and just so perfect together. They make me believe in love and hope that one day I find what they have.

My phone rings again, and this time it's the security door downstairs. "Hello," I greet.

"Hey, darlin'," Blake greets.

"Come on up," I tell him and press the button to unlock the door.

I grab the jean jacket I pulled out to take in case we're outside and it gets cool with the breeze. I make sure my cross-body purse has my ChapStick, sunglasses, keys, and slip my phone in as well. Just as I'm zipping it up, there is a knock at my door.

I unlock the deadbolt and open the door where Blake is on the other side, dressed in a pair of what I'd call golfing shorts and a polo. Nothing too fancy, but also not too casual. He holds out a beautiful bouquet of fall flowers, wrapped in a beautiful paper. They look like they came straight from a farmer and not the average florists.

"Thank you. These are beautiful. Where did you find them?" I ask as I step back so he can enter my condo.

"I stopped at the farmer's market before I headed over here," he tells me as he leans in and kisses my cheek.

"Let me get them into some water," I say as I step into the kitchen. He follows and watches as I rummage through a few cabinets looking for the vase I know I brought with me. I finally locate it, and after adding some water, I put in the plant food and then add the flowers. Once they are arranged, I set the vase in the center of my counter so I can see them from multiple rooms.

I turn around and wrap my arms around Blake. "Thank you. They are perfect." He wraps his large arms around me, holding me tight against his body.

"Anytime. You look gorgeous today, by the way. I like this dress on you," he says beside my ear. The gruffness of his voice, mixed with his breath on my exposed skin thanks to my hair being pulled up has my body reacting in ways I can't control.

"Thank you. I think my belly popped a little more overnight," I tell him as I step back and rub a hand down my bump.

"I'd say so. Do you mind?" he asks and holds his hand out. I nod, giving him the green light to touch my belly. I don't know why that gesture makes me feel so good, but the fact he thought to ask before just touching me tells me a lot about the man that he is.

"Hey, baby, I'm your daddy. I hope you're being good to your momma."

"So far so good," I assure him.

"You ready to get going? I have a few things planned for our day," Blake tells me.

"I'm ready!" I tell him. I grab my jacket and purse off the counter and follow him to the door, which he opens for me and lets me exit first. He pulls it closed, and steps aside so I can lock it up.

As we make our way to the elevator, Blake grabs my hand and links our fingers together. I love the feel of his big hand surrounding mine. The elevator opens as soon as we hit the button, and the ride down is quick. Blake escorts me outside and to his SUV. "Decided to dive the bigger car today, hmm?"

"Yep, I like mixing it up. Plus I wanted you to see it and approve that it is suitable for a car seat for the baby."

"Definitely passes the car seat requirement," I tell him as we both buckle in. "Where are we headed first?" I ask as he pulls out of the parking lot.

"I figured we'd start the day with lunch. Are you hungry?" he asks.

"I am. I had a small breakfast a few hours ago, so lunch sounds perfect." I tell him.

We fill the drive to the restaurant with small talk. He fills me in on his practice and game schedule for the next week. They are headed out of town later in the week and will be gone for five nights. I fill him in on my schedule and Tess plans to come next weekend.

We pull up to a cute little café looking place. From the looks of it, this place is popular, probably with the Sunday brunch crowd. "Is this okay?" Blake asks before he turns off the SUV.

"Looks perfect to me. I'm not super picky," I assure him.

We make our way to the hostess stand and give Blake gives her his name. She assures us it won't be more than ten minutes to be seated, so we step aside and continue our small talk until his name is called and we're taken to a table on their patio. The view is amazing from here, and I take a moment to soak it all in.

"Good afternoon. I'm Katie and I'll be taking care of you today. What can I get the two of you to drink? We've got our bottomless mimosas for twenty-two ninety-nine, or bottomless Bloody Mary's for the same."

"Do you have any flavored lemonades?" I ask and pat my belly. "As good as a mimosa sounds right now, no alcohol for me." I smile.

"We do! We muddle our own fruits, so we can make

you any flavor you'd like! My favorite is the black rasp-berry. It is a mixture of black berries and raspberries," Katie tells me.

"That does sound good. I'll try that one," I tell her then look at the menu.

"I'm good with water," Blake tells her.

"Lemon?" she asks.

"Sure, that'd be great," he replies.

"I'll be back shortly with your drinks." She smiles before turning away so we can decide on our meals.

"Did you want to order or do the brunch line? I'm happy either way," Blake asks.

"The brunch option looks great, so I'm good with that," I tell him. Katie returns and we both let her know we'll do brunch. Once she leaves again, we both get up to get our food from the many options they have set out.

"This place is so good. Have you been here before?" I ask Blake after a few bites of my food.

"A few times. Ryker's wife, Avery, loves this place, so I've been here with them a handful of times."

"Who on the team do you hang out with the most?"

"Ryker, Aiden, and Tristan, for the most part. Damien a little more since last season, especially after he met Trinity."

"Camden always had a small group of teammates that he was constantly with. It almost felt like I had that many more brothers growing up." I laugh, remem-bering those years.

"I can only imagine. Must have been hard having so many guys trying to protect you."

"Eh, it wasn't the worst. Except when they'd try to run off my actual boyfriend."

Blake laughs. "I hope he didn't run away."

"He expected it, so he didn't back down. I think they respected him more because of that."

"Yep, if a guy goes running from the brothers how the hell is he going to stand up for his girl if the need arises?"

"I'd never thought of it like that," I admit.

"Guys might not always express why they do things, especially as teenagers, but we usually have a method to our madness."

We continue our conversation as we both dig into our food. It flows so easily between the two of us, like we've known each other forever, which is refreshing to say the least.

"Are you ready for the next stop on our day together?" Blake asks as after he's paid the check from lunch.

"I am. Any clues as to where we're off to next?" I ask, batting my eyelashes at him in hopes that he'll tell me.

He taps the tip of my nose. "You're really adorable when you do that, but it isn't going to work." He smirks and I somewhat wish I could just kiss the look right off his handsome face. If batting my eyelashes isn't going to work, maybe pouting will, so I do just that. "Still not going to work." He laughs. "But I do like the effort.

Come on, let's go." He stands up and offers his hand to help me up.

I return my facial expression to a smile and accept his hand. Once I'm standing, he entwines his fingers with mine and I love the feeling of being claimed by Blake.

He leads me out of the restaurant and to his car. I hear the locks click just before Blake opens the passenger door. He finally lets go of my hand so I can slide into the seat. He waits for me to get settled and buckle my seatbelt before closing the door and rounding the front and getting in behind the wheel.

My stomach has butterflies flittering with nerves as Bake pulls out into traffic. I have no idea where he's taking me, and it is driving me crazy with anticipation. I secretly love that he's keeping me on my toes and surprising me with today's plans-- not that I'll ever admit that to him.

We pull into a large shopping district. It has a large mall on one end, but also multiple standalone stores and some smaller strip malls spread out in the different parking lot areas. Blake drives around until we're in front of a large baby store. When he parks the car, I turn in my seat, ready to question him.

"I thought we could go in and look at baby stuff. We're going to need to set up a nursery or two. Maybe start the registry. I know my mother is going to want to start buying things right away, so it would be helpful to know what you want."

Tears prick the back of my eyes. I've done a little

research on brands for different things, but hadn't gone into a baby store, unless you count the baby section at Target. "I'd love to," I choke out.

"If you aren't ready, we can table this until later." Blake cups my cheek and wipes at my tears.

"No, I want to go in. These are happy tears," I assure him. "Just these damn pregnancy hormones have me crying at the drop of a hat. Or apparently by parking outside a baby store." I laugh a watery laugh.

"Okay, let's go see what kind of damage we can do," Blake suggests.

As soon as we walk into the store, Blake leads me over to the kiosk that has a large sign above it which reads Baby Registry. He taps the tablet screen and proceeds to enter the information to set up a new account. Once all the pertinent information is entered and the registry is created, the instructions tell us to take the scanning gun and start scanning items and it will add them to the list. I snag the scanner and walk deeper into the store. Blake grabs a shopping cart to bring along.

"Maybe we'll find something we can't live without today," he says as he giddily pushes it along.

We walk up and down every aisle. From pacifiers to car seats, we check out every contraption known to man that is in this store for babies. "Who knew babies could need so much stuff," I muse to Blake as we look down yet another aisle.

"You don't need even half the stuff they sell in this store," a very pregnant lady says from where she stands just a few feet away. "Don't get sucked into all the gimmicky products. I promise you, they are a waste of your money," she adds.

"Thank you, it is a little overwhelming if I'm honest," I tell her.

"This is baby number three for me, and at this point, all I need is diapers, clothes, a baby wrap or carrier for when you need your hands but baby doesn't want to be put down, a car seat, and maybe some bottles if you are going to bottle feed."

"Good to know. This is our first little one, and our first time here, so going a little crazy adding things to the list," Blake tells her as he rubs his hand on my belly. Those butterflies flip flop at how he says *our first*, like we're planning on having more kids in the future.

"Congratulations," the lady says as she places the bottles she was looking at in her basket and leaves us to continue shopping.

"Aww, look at how cute this is." I stop and hold up a onesie. The top says *Hi, I'm new here!* across the front.

"We should get it. Looks gender neutral to me, so can work either way." Blake suggests. I've been hesitant to add anything to the basket, but he's right. It would work no matter if we're having a boy or girl.

I hesitate, wondering if I should. I don't know why buying something right now feels like I'm jinxing anything, but Blake must realize my hesitation.

"Talk to me." He closes the distance between us, turning me to face him and tips my chin up so I'm looking into his eyes. The ones that I find so damn comforting. His eyes on me brings this calmness over me. I don't know how he does it, but just one look and I'm like putty in his hands.

"It just feels strange to buy something so early. What if something goes wrong?" I ask, my voice barely above a whisper.

"Has anything happened to give you the indication that something might be wrong?" he asks.

"No, my OB said everything looked perfect the last time I saw her. I don't go to see my new one for a few more weeks."

"Will you tell me when that is so I can go with you?" he asks.

"You want to go?" I ask, a little shocked.

"Of course. I told you I'd be here every step of the way. As long as you are okay with me being there and I'm available, I'd like to go."

"Okay, I'll send you the appointment details."

"And I can share my schedule with you so you know when I have practice, games, and travel so you can hopefully book around those. I know it won't always be possible, but I'd like to be there as often as possible."

"I'll see what I can do. I only go monthly for now, so should be pretty easy to work around. As I get further along, I'll have to start going more often."

"I'll do my best to be there. That goes for regular check-ups, tours of the hospital, birthing classes. Whatever you want to do, I'll be there."

"Thank you," I tell him before I wrap my arms

around his body. He does the same, engulfing me in a tight hug. When he kisses the top of my head, I almost lose control and tip my head up so he can kiss me on the lips. Instead, I step back, breaking our connection.

I place the onesie that is still in my hand into the basket and move forward to the next display.

CHAPTER 13
BLAKE

TODAY'S DATE HAS BEEN THE BEST IDEA I'VE HAD IN A long ass time. We spent a few hours in the baby store, having fun looking at all the things companies have made for raising babies. We ended up leaving the store with the onesie Raven picked out, a package of newborn diapers, wipes, and some burp cloths. Nothing huge, but the registry is chock full of all kinds of things.

"Are you still good to go, or do I need to cancel our next stop?" I ask Raven as we place the bags in the back of my SUV.

"I'm good, especially if we can stop for a late afternoon Starbucks," she says.

"That we can do," I assure her as we both get into the car. We aren't going far, just over to another building in this shopping complex, but it's far enough that we drive across the parking lot. She's in luck, because halfway to our next stop is a Starbucks, so I pull into the drive through. We both place our orders and I pull forward.

With our drinks and her slice of coffee cake, I drive us over to the nail salon. I booked us pedicures. I figured it was a great way to relax after a few hours walking around shopping.

"I thought we could get pedicures together," I say as I turn off the engine.

"How did you plan all of this?" she asks, a little shocked.

I shrug. "Just tried to think of casual things you might enjoy," I tell her honestly.

We make our way into the nail salon, and they whisk us back to two chairs that are side by side. They both have the water already filling up the little tubs. Once we both settled into our chairs, the massage setting turned on, the employee hands Raven a book filled with all the color options she can pick from.

"Hmm, I don't know what to go with," she says as she flips through all the pages. They have practically every shade imaginable.

"What's your favorite color?" I ask, knowing this is another nugget of information I can tuck away.

"Purple," she quickly says. I look over the purples and point at one. It's a little on the dark side but screams Raven to me.

"Are you a mind reader?" She chuckles. "That was one of the colors I was thinking about."

"It reminds me of you," I tell her.

She tells the employee that it is the color she wants, and they go and pull it from their wall of colors.

We keep our conversation light as we both enjoy the next hour. My pedicure ends before hers since I'm not getting polish, but I stay sitting next to her as they expertly paint her toes, even adding a design to her big toes.

"Feel good?" I ask once we're ready to leave.

"So good. Thank you for this. It was just what I needed before returning to work tomorrow."

"How about some dinner before we call it a night?" I suggest. "We can grab some take out and head back to your place or mine, whatever you prefer."

"That sounds perfect," she agrees and she doesn't hesitate when I slip my hand around hers, entwining our fingers together as we walk out to the parking lot.

I carry up the bags of food in one hand and the baby purchases in the other. We decided on Mexican food from a place that wasn't far from the nail salon. We stop and put in the to go order, then take it to Raven's condo.

"Would you like something to drink?" she asks as she pulls out two plates, then silverware for both of us.

"Sure, what do you have?" I ask.

She sets the plates down on the small table and returns to the kitchen, where she opens the fridge. "I've got raspberry lemonade, water, club soda, or milk. Sorry, I know it isn't much of a selection. We should have grabbed you something before we came here."

"I don't drink much but water and protein shakes

during the season, so it doesn't take much to impress me. I'll just have a glass of water."

Raven hands me a glass filled with ice water, then pours herself a glass of raspberry lemonade before joining me at the table. We open the large containers, taking some of each to fill our plates.

"This is so good," she says before taking another bite of the steak and shrimp fajitas we're sharing.

"I agree," I say, before taking my own bite. "I'll have to go back to this place; I'd never been there before."

"So, what will your work schedule look like most weeks?" I ask.

"Pretty normal business hours. If I don't have court or client meetings, I'm usually in the office between eight and nine and done no later than five. Most courts finish up or go into recess by mid-to-late afternoon, or at least the judges I mainly dealt with in Anaheim. I can only hope they are the same way here."

"Maybe we can get dinner this week before I leave on my trip?"

"When are you guys leaving?" I ask.

"Early afternoon on Wednesday. We play Thursday night in Toronto, then Buffalo on Saturday night, in New Jersey Sunday, and finally back home on Monday."

"That's a busy trip," Raven raises her brows at me.

"It is, but just how it goes. I'm kind of surprised it is only three games. Usually when we go all the way out east like that, we are gone for two weeks and hit up more of the teams."

"Camden always said it was easier on the body once he'd been in a time zone for a few days, and I can see how that would make sense. Especially when you're going from the west coast to the east coast."

"It can be hard on the body, that's for sure. I'm on such a specific routine, and when my internal clock is three hours off, it can make for an interesting time. But it is something every team and player has to deal with and figure out how to overcome. We spend half our season on the road, so it isn't like this is new. Home ice advantage has more than just your home building in your favor. It can also be things like the time zone and whether that play in your favor."

"I never thought of those other factors making a difference, but I can see how they could."

"How we all play, how healthy we stay, especially when we get deeper into the season, every little thing can change the outcome of the game."

We clean up from dinner and have enough leftovers for Raven to take with her tomorrow for lunch. "Are you sure you don't want to take the leftovers?" she asks as she boxes them up into some Tupperware.

"You take it. I'll probably just eat at the practice facility. We have a chef and food at our disposal."

"Must be nice being a professional athlete," she teases.

"Perks are definitely nice," I wink.

I check the time and see that it is already almost eight-thirty. I know she needs to get to bed at an early hour tonight so she's ready for her big day tomorrow.

"I should probably get out of your hair so you can get to bed early."

Raven eyes flick to the large clock on her wall, then back to mine. I can't quite put my finger on what I see in her eyes, but it is something.

"Okay. Thank you for today. I had a great time. Everything was perfect. From the flowers you brought me, to take out together. I loved every second of it."

"I'm glad you enjoyed it; I had a great time with you. So, dinner Tuesday?" I ask circling back to my earlier question.

"Yes, just text me and we can figure out when and where."

"Sounds like a plan."

We both walk toward her door but neither of us reach out to open it. We're stuck in a trance, staring at each other to see who will break first.

I take a half step, closing the distance between our bodies. I slide a hand over her bump, resting it on the side. It feels like it is harder on this side, so it makes me wonder if the baby is laying there or what exactly I'm feeling. I cup Raven's face with my other hand, loving the feeling of her skin under my fingertips. "Good night, darlin'. I'll see you soon," I say before lowering my face and brushing a chaste kiss across her lips. I know we're taking things slower, but I just couldn't resist the moment. The little gasp that falls from Raven's lips tells me she enjoyed it and wants more just as much as I do.

"Night, Blake," she whispers as I take a step back. I

reach around and open the door, knowing that if I don't leave now, things are going to take a big ole step back into sexy town, and I know she wants to stay away from that for now.

"Lock up behind me, and get a good night's sleep," I say from the other side of the threshold.

"Will do," she says as I start walking backwards towards the stairwell. I take the stairs two at a time, forcing my body to move further and further away from her so that I don't just turn around and go get my girl.

Once in my car, my mind is so focused on replaying today's events and my time spent with Raven that I don't even notice the music on in the background, nor do I really notice the traffic. It's like I'm on autopilot when I pull into my driveway.

I park in the garage, then get out. I quickly walk the trash cans down to the end of my driveway, so they'll be emptied tomorrow morning when the trucks come through. On my way back up, I pull my phone from my pocket to shoot Raven a text message before she heads to bed.

> Had a great time today. I can't wait to see you on Tuesday night. Decide what you want for dinner and I'll make it happen. I hope your first day goes well tomorrow. If you want to celebrate after work, you know how to find me. {Winky face}

> Also, I made it home.

I'm just about to get into bed. Not sure if I'll fall asleep anytime soon thanks to the nerves for tomorrow.

I know a great way to make you sleepy. {Devilish smirk}

{eye roll} How did I know that is exactly what you'd say? LOL

{shoulder shrug} Can't blame a guy for trying.

{blushing emoji}

Are you wet for me, darlin'?

Blake! Friends. Remember?

Doesn't mean I can't make you wet. I can't get the memory of your sweet pussy wrapped around my cock out of my mind. I get off to it frequently.

{panting emoji}

Do I need to call you and walk you through an orgasm?

The text bubbles pop up and dance across my screen like she's typing a freaking novel. I watch them bounce as I make my way up to my room. I locked up as I came inside, so heading straight to my bed is on my mind now. My cock is already hard and pressing against my zipper, ready to be let free.

I toss my phone on the bed and notice the bubbles have disappeared. She must have deleted what she was typing. I know I'm pushing the envelope, but fuck, I can't get her out of my mind.

Once I'm stripped down to nothing but my boxers, I adjust my cock and take a seat, settling against the headboard. I grab my phone and mull over what to say.

> I'm sorry if that was over the line. I promise to be good and roll back the sex talk and advances. I didn't mean to offend you if that was too brash.

The bubbles reappear, and finally a text comes through.

> I get it. The chemistry between us is strong. Multiple times today, I found myself wishing I could just push up and kiss you after you'd done something sweet. I really like you, Blake, and hope that whatever this is between us isn't a fluke. I know I said I wanted space and time, but after today, I don't really think that is true anymore.

I read her words twice, making sure I don't misunderstand what she's saying. I can't help the smile that tugs at my lips as I let everything sink in. I hit the Face-Time icon, needing to see her beautiful face right fucking now.

"Hi," she greets as her face fills my phone's screen. Her face is void of makeup and she's still the most beautiful woman I've seen.

"Hey, darlin'," I drawl. "I'm here to tell you that you

can kiss me anytime you want. I definitely won't object to that."

"Is that so?" She smiles at me like she's smitten.

"Anytime, anywhere," I confirm. "What do you say I pick you up after work. We can grab some dinner and spend the night together. Better yet, pack an overnight bag and you can stay at my place the next two nights until I have to leave for our away series." I know my offer is bold, but why prolong what we both want?

Raven chews on her bottom lip and I want nothing more than to kiss and suck on that very spot. "Yes," she says, and I jump up, my free hand making a fist as I pump it in the air.

"Fuck, yes!" I cheer. "Be ready for me, darlin', because tomorrow night you are mine." I wink.

"You are incorrigible." She laughs, and it is like music to my soul.

"Only when it comes to you," I tell her as I drop back down onto my bed. "So, about that orgasm," I bounce my eyebrows and smirk.

"Incorrigible." She laughs. "And insatiable it seems."

"I'll never get my fill of you," I tell her honestly, because I won't. Not after a day, week, month, year, decade or century. I want this woman for eternity. Don't ask me how I know that, but I can feel it deep down. Fate might have brought us together that night in Vegas, and again when she showed up at my game, I'm not about to chance fate and let her get away ever again.

CHAPTER 14
RAVEN

I SIT AT MY DESK, OVERWHELMED IN A GOOD WAY AT HOW amazing being back to work in my new office is. The staff at this location are all hard working and were so welcoming. My assistant, Brenda, has been in my office most of the day, helping me get caught up on the case files that were assigned to me by other partners. While we don't often hand off cases we're already in the middle of, they transferred some newer ones that hadn't had much work done on them yet and were easy to give to me.

"I say we call it a day. How about you?" I say to Brenda.

"We've had quite the day; I agree it is a good stopping point. Plus, my husband will be happy to have me home early for once." Brenda smiles at me from across my desk. She's got probably fifteen, maybe twenty years on me, and has that comforting mother vibe going for her. I knew within minutes we were going to work well together, and that feeling has been solidified after today.

"Do you have any plans tonight?" I ask.

"Just dinner together before he leaves for work. He on nights this week."

"Oh, well, don't let me keep you. Get on home and enjoy your time together before he's off to work," I tell her.

"You don't have to tell me twice." She stands and tucks her pen into the spirals of her notebook. "Do you have any plans?" she asks as she straightens the chair she was sitting in.

"Just dinner with a friend," I say. I haven't divulged anything about Blake and me yet. I did tell her I'm expecting and when I'm due since that will be important for cases I'm assigned.

"Well, have fun. I'll see you tomorrow morning." She gives a little finger wave before exiting my office. I turn my attention back to my computer and shoot off a few emails to my old assistant and one of the attorneys in the office I left who had taken over some of my cases.

Once my emails are taken care of, I shut down my computer and gather my things. I check to make sure I haven't missed any text messages. My notifications are empty, so I tap on Blake's name to shoot him a message.

> Hey, just about to walk out of work. Are we still on for tonight? Did you still want me to pack a bag?

As long as that's what you want. Like I said last night, I'm ready to do this, but will go at whatever pace you want to go at.

I'm headed home to grab my stuff. Will you be home in an hour? I'm guessing with traffic it will be at least that long.

I'm home now. What do you want for dinner? I can make us something or we can order in.

I've had a craving all day for some shrimp alfredo.

Say no more. Drive safe and I'll see you when you get here. Anything specific you'd like me to pick up for you to have here? Snacks? Breakfast items? Drinks?

You're the best {kissy face} I love to snack on fancy cheese and crackers, can't go wrong with some ice cream – classic vanilla, especially if you have caramel sauce – and for breakfast, I've been on a scrambled eggs and toast kick lately.

Got it.

See you soon.

I drop my phone into my purse as I walk out to my car. The sun is shining and feels great on my face as I open the door to my car. I slip inside my car and slide my sunglasses onto my nose. It doesn't take long before

I'm pulling out into traffic. I inch along with everyone else trying to make it home. This is one part of my day that I usually dread, but I don't find myself being upset about it today, and I think that has to do with a certain man I'll be seeing just as soon as I can make it home, pack a bag, and drive over to his place.

As soon as I enter my place, I kick off my heels. I don't wear super high ones, but they are starting to kill my feet. I'm probably going to need to put some new work shoes on my ever-growing shopping list. Not only do I have tons of baby things to buy, but also pregnancy related. I take off my slacks and dress top, changing into some comfortable lounge pants and a baggy sweatshirt.

Are you cooking or are we going out? I just changed into some lounge wear but can change again if we're going somewhere.

Wear whatever is comfortable. I'm cooking you dinner, darlin'.

A man after my own heart.

Damn straight. How long until you are on your way? No rush, just want to time having food ready when you get here.

I should be out of here in the next ten, maybe twenty minutes. I can shoot you a text if that would help? Traffic was a bitch getting home, so it might take me a little bit to get to your place.

Send me a text. Drive safe.

I pull out a weekender size bag and start adding pj's, clothes for work, after work clothes, my toiletries, makeup, and lastly, toss my kindle into the bag. I remember to grab my chargers and toss them into the bag as well. I know if I forget something, I can just drive back home, but I'd prefer not to have to do that tonight.

I take one last look around and don't see anything I might have forgotten, so back out to my car I go.

> On my way.

I text and send him the link to my ETA, that way he can track and see how traffic is slowing me down.

> See ya soon, darlin'

The giddy feeling amps up as I drive to his house. The large gate opens and I'm waved through by the security guards manning it at the opening of his subdivision.

I wind through the streets and love the peacefulness of this neighborhood. I can see the appeal of living here. Everyone's property is so well maintained and land-scaped. Inviting street lamps light up driveways and the pathways to the front doors. I pull into Blake's driveway and find him leaning against the pillar on the front porch. He motions for me to pull into the garage stall he's opened up and I do just that.

Before I can open my door, it is opened for me. "Hi," his deep voice greets.

"Hi," I say as I slip my hand into his. He assists as I slip out of the driver's seat and stand up. His arms wrap around my torso as he hauls me against his chest. My head tips up and our lips instantly find each other. The kiss is light, natural, like we've greeted one another like this for ages.

"We should get inside; I don't want to ruin dinner." Blake says as he pulls back from the kiss.

"Yeah," I say as a sigh leaves my lips.

"Just the one bag?" he asks as he holds it up after removing it from the back seat.

"Yes," I confirm.

Blake leads me inside the house and sets my bag on the stairs. He immediately leads us into the kitchen, which smells so good.

"Food should be done in just a couple of minutes," he says as he stirs the large pan.

"What did you make?" I ask as I take a seat on one of the bar stools that line his island.

"Shrimp alfredo, garlic bread, a Caesar salad, and I bought brownies and some ice cream for dessert." He smiles proudly.

"You made shrimp alfredo? Like from scratch?"

"Yep." He pops the p. "All from scratch. Well, I didn't make the pasta myself, but I made the sauce and put it all together."

"You really are the whole package," I murmur.

"I'm here to please." He leans down and presses a chaste kiss to my lips.

A timer goes off and he steps away. I watch as he

pulls a pan out of the oven with garlic bread on it. The buttery garlic aromas waft my way and make my stomach growl in anticipation.

"I take it you're hungry?" Blake chuckles as he moves the bread to a cutting board and starts slicing.

"Just a little," I reply. "Can I help with anything?" I offer.

"Nope, just sit your cute little butt there and let me take care of you." He tosses a smile over his shoulder. I don't miss the way his eyes smolder as he looks at me. I find myself needing to squeeze my thighs together, seeking some friction.

Blake places the garlic bread on a plate, and sets it on the counter between where I'm sitting and the seat next to me. He returns to the stove, stirs the pan of pasta and turns off the burner. He carries it over and places it down on a hot pad, then steps away to grab two plates, along with silverware for both of us. "Can I get you something to drink?" he asks as he sets down the plates and silverware.

"That'd be great. What do you have?" I ask.

"Water, lemonade, milk. I think I have some sodas in the garage, and some beers, which I realize you can't have," he offers.

"Some lemonade would be great." I smile and answer him.

I watch as he grabs two glasses and adds some ice to them before opening the fridge and pulling out a brand new container of my favorite lemonade.

"How did you know?" I ask.

"You mentioned it yesterday," he says as he hands me one of the glasses. I take a drink before setting it on the counter. "Ladies first." He motions to the large pan of Alfredo. I take a serving, going back in to take a few extra shrimp, then add two slices of the garlic bread to my plate. I also take a small serving of salad. It's been hit or miss for me since finding out I was pregnant.

"Oh my god," I say behind my hand as my mouth is half full. "This is the best I've ever tasted. Who taught you to cook?"

Blake laughs. "I'm glad you like it. This recipe happens to be my grandmother's. I'd cook with her whenever I was at their house, which was often."

"That's so sexy," I tell him.

"That I cooked with my grandmother?" He raises a brow in question.

"No," I laugh, "Just that you cook in general. I love that you've kept her recipe and use them in your own home. I assume you'll pass them down to our child one day."

"I never wanted to be dependent on food services or takeout all the time. Food is important to athletes. I figured out at a young age what I put in my body affects the output I could give on the ice. So, cooking became an intricate part of my routine. While it sucks to cook for just one usually, during the season, I eat the equivalent of a couple adults, so it all works out," he tells me.

"That makes sense," I tell him as I devour my plate.

"Not a Caesar fan?" he asks as I push the salad around.

"I usually love them, but this little gumdrop isn't the biggest fan," I explain.

"Ah, yes, I was reading that women can have cravings but also aversions to foods while pregnant."

"You were reading?"

"Yeah, I bought a book on pregnancy. I figured it was probably a good idea to brush up on what you're going through. Might help me be a better partner and help you through it as best as I can."

I put my fork down and turn so I'm facing Blake. He does the same. "I think that is the sweetest thing. Thank you for being so willing to take this on with me. It really releases some of the stress I was starting to feel. I had no idea how I was going to do everything as a single mom."

Blake tips my chin up and cups my cheek. "You won't have to do one damn thing by yourself. I'm ready to take the next step. Be by your side. Be right there whenever you or this baby needs me. We'll have to learn how to balance my schedule during the season, but I promise you there are other women who can help you through all of it. They're like one big secondary family. I'll have to introduce you sooner than later."

Blake leans in and presses his lips to mine before I can reply. The kiss is tender and slow. I open for him when his tongue slides across the seam of my lips and he deepens the kiss further. We make out like two teenagers left alone for a few minutes.

"Finish up and we can resume this later," he says after we break apart. He presses a kiss to the corner of my mouth before sitting back in his chair and turning back to his food.

We talk as we both finish. I grab one last slice of the garlic bread because it is just that good—my breath be dammed. Once we're both stuffed, I help him clean up the kitchen so that it goes faster, much to his dismay.

"We can relax out back, in the living room, or upstairs-- your choice," Blake says once the dishwasher is running and all the pans have been hand washed, dried, and put away.

"Such good options," I muse. Blake wraps his arms around me from behind, lining up his front to my back. I don't miss his half hard cock that presses against my ass. He slides his hands over my belly, resting his large paws on either side of my belly. His fingers overlap one another in the center.

I relax back into him, feeling so comfortable as he surrounds me completely. "I like this," I say as a yawn slips out.

"I have the perfect idea then," he says as he grabs my hand and links our fingers. I stumble a few steps as I right myself, following him as he leads me through the house. After verifying all the doors are shut and locked, he grabs my bag and carries it upstairs. We go into his room, where he drops my hand from his, and motions toward his closet and bathroom. "I made some space for your things," he says, as he walks through a door. I follow and find him placing my bag down on a little seat in the closet. This room is huge, possibly bigger than my entire bedroom in my condo.

"Holy bejesus," I say as I spin in a circle. There are multiple empty shelves and hanging sections.

"It's a little overkill for just me, so feel free to use as much of it as you wish," he says.

I open my bag and start pulling things out. "Can you place these by the bed?" I ask, handing over my charger cords for my phone and tablets.

"Of course," he says, taking them and heading back into the bedroom. I empty out my clothes, hanging up my work ones on the rod and placing the folded ones on the empty shelf. I take my toiletries into the bathroom, setting them up as nicely as I can on the counter. I don't want him to think I'm taking over with all my products.

"That's all you have?" he asks as he pokes his head in to see what I'm doing.

"Yeah, I didn't need to bring everything," I tell him.

"You're welcome to bring whatever you want and leave it here if you'd like. I kind of like having you in my space," he tells me.

I walk out of the bathroom and right into his open arms. The way this man makes me feel so protected and loved is like nothing I've ever experienced with someone else. It's scary to think that we can be so compatible after such a short time.

"Are you ready for bed, or did you need to change again?" he asks.

"I brought some actual pj's. I'd be sweltering hot

wearing these to bed." I look down and tug at the lounge pants I have on.

"You're welcome to sleep in your birthday suit." Blake wags his eyebrows at me, and I can't help but laugh.

"I'm sure you'd just love that." I laugh.

"Abso-fucking-lutely." He grins. "I'd join you in the party."

I dip back into the closet and grab my pj's- a pair of small shorts and a tank top. I wasn't lying when I said I swelter at night. This baby has made me a furnace these past few weeks.

Blake whistles as I enter the bedroom, my legs on full display, my nipples as well now that I've taken off my bra. I'm sure I look a hot mess, but you wouldn't know it by the smoldering look I'm getting from Blake.

"Come here," he growls, his finger crooking in a come here motion. I walk toward him, a little slowly, mainly to drive him a little bit crazy until I'm just a few inches from him.

"You're the most gorgeous woman I've ever laid my eyes on," he says, his hands resting now on my hips. "I don't know what I did to deserve a chance with you but fuck, if I'm going to let it pass me by." He tugs me closer, closing those few inches of space we had lingering between us. Blake tips my chin up with one hand as the other slowly sides under my tank top, his calloused fingers tickling along my skin as he slides it up to my extremely sensitive breasts.

"Whoa," I cry out as his thumb swipes over my nipple.

"You okay?" he asks, slightly pulling back, but not completely removing his hand from under my shirt.

"Just sensitive," I assure him.

"You tell me if anything is too much," he instructs, and I just nod before his lips capture mine in a searing kiss.

Blake brings the hand that was cupping my cheek down and wraps it around my back, lifting me off my feet. He walks me over to the bed, setting me down on the edge, all while never breaking our kiss. I lay back, pulling him with me as I go. He follows me down onto the mattress, his body now covering mine as he pins me underneath him. The feeling of his body against mine brings back so many memories from our previous time together. It's what I've craved, what I've needed. I don't know why I thought I needed to resist this.

CHAPTER 15
BLAKE

We lay in bed, both sated and relaxed after a ravishing round of sex. Neither one of us could get enough of the other. Raven has her head resting on my chest as I run a hand up and down her back. Her skin is smooth under my callused fingers. "I'm going to miss you so fucking much this week," I say, breaking the silence we'd fallen into.

"The feeling is mutual. I'm going to miss you as well. I can already tell I'm not going to be a fan of you on the road all the time," she says as she shifts so she can look up at me. "It's definitely a different feeling missing you versus missing Camden."

I love her like this-- makeup free, relaxed, in my arms and in my bed . I can definitely get used to this every night.

I chuckle lightly. "I imagine it is, but it's a fact of my life and not one I can change."

"I know, and I'd never ask you to give up your

career. I know you don't make it to this level if you don't love it and put in the work required."

"Are you busy next Saturday?" I ask.

"No. Well, at least I don't think I am," she replies.

"There is a team BBQ. Families are welcome. It's a casual event that the owner, Nathan, hosts every year, and I'd like for you to attend with me if that's something you're comfortable doing," I state.

"Do all the guys know the details surrounding us?" she asks.

"Yes." I don't lie to her. I never would. "And there is absolutely no judgment from any of them. I'm sure all of their wives are just itching to meet you. They like to bring every new girlfriend into the fold."

"Girlfriend," she says, the word sounding foreign on her tongue. "Is that what I am?" she questions.

I shift so I'm looking down at her. This is a defining moment in whatever this is between the two of us. "I know it's been a whirlwind, but you can't deny the connection we have. I know neither of us wants to rush things, but I also know I don't want to let you go, Raven. So, yes, I'm asking you to do this with me, as my girlfriend. Let's see where this goes between us as a couple." I hold my breath, waiting for her response.

"Breathe," she laughs as she taps on my chest before sliding her hand up and around my neck so she can pull me down to her. I let out the air trapped in my lungs and suck in a new breath just before she whispers, "Yes," then seals her lips to mine.

I roll her completely under me, my cock already

hard and aching once again. I need to be inside her as soon as possible. I deepen the kiss as I reach down between her thighs and find her wet and ready for me. I slip two fingers inside her pussy and find that sensitive spot that has her quickly on edge.

I pull away from her lips, dropping kisses on her neck and chest. "I need to be inside you, now," I growl into her skin.

"What are you waiting for then?" she asks as she opens her thighs wider.

I grip my cock, stroking my hand over it, coating it with her arousal. I line my cock up with her entrance and thrust inside. We both cry out in pleasure as I'm fully seated. Her body pulses around my shaft. I give her a few moments, then start to move. I press my forehead against hers as I make love to her. My thrusts are at a punishingly slow pace but are just as powerful as fast and hard ones. Both our orgasms are building, and I can tell by the way her pussy starts to flutter around my cock that she's getting close. "Tell me what you need, darlin'," I whisper before kissing her.

"More," she says between breaths.

I pick up the speed ever so slightly, adding a little power to each thrust, making sure when our pelvises connect, they apply direct pressure to her clit.

"Yes!" she cries out, her body shaking now. "Don't stop," she chants as her eyes start to roll back in her head.

I push my body up, gripping her hips as I pick up my pace, my hips snapping back and forth like I'm about to come undone. She detonates, coating my cock in her release, which triggers my own. I slam through the vice like grip and bury myself as deep inside her as I can possibly get. My balls empty every last drop of cum they can inside her.

"If I wasn't already pregnant, I think I would be after that," she chuckles once we both come down from our orgasms.

"We can't hurt the baby with sex can we?" I ask, suddenly worried that I overdid things.

"No, sex is perfectly fine to have all the way to the end, unless I was to be put on pelvic rest for some reason. And before you get worried about that, I've had no indications of any issues this entire time. If it would make you feel any better, you can come to my next doctor appointment and ask my OB any of your burning questions," she says.

"When is that?" I ask.

"Since I've had to transfer my care, I have a new patient appointment two weeks from Wednesday."

I mentally go over my schedule. I believe we'll be gone then, which irritates me, but there isn't much I can do about our travel schedule. "I think I'm gone that day," I say as I reach for my phone on the side table. I pull up the schedule and sure enough, we're playing in Chicago that night. "Fuck," I mutter.

"It's okay if you can't make that one. It shouldn't be an exciting one. I'll pee in a cup. They'll measure my belly and ask me some questions, probably a few more than normal since this is my first time with this office, but nothing to be of concern with, and then send me on my way until next month."

"Do you already have that appointment booked?" I ask.

"No, but I can do my best to make it for when you can come. If it isn't a game day, what time of day is best for you?"

"First thing in the morning or later afternoon, but I can make anytime work. Coach is understanding for the most part."

"I try for first thing as well, that way my day isn't split. That, and I've found the earlier in the day I go in, the less likely they are to be backed up and behind."

"Do you want me to share my calendar with you?" I offer. "One of the office people created a google calendar with all our practices, games, and travel info."

"Sure, that might be helpful," she agrees.

I copy the link and text it to her. That way she can add it to her calendar. "Done," I say before putting my phone away. "How about a shower before sleep?" I suggest now that we're both sweaty and messy.

"I suppose you can convince me to go stand in that enormous shower you have. I've been dreaming about what that rainfall shower head will feel like."

"You can use it whenever your little heart desires," I say before kissing her lips. I scoop her up into my arms and carry her into the bathroom. I set Raven down on the countertop so I can turn the water on and get it nice and steamy before we step in.

"Fuck, that's cold," she yelps as she jumps off the counter, laughing as she does.

"Sorry, darlin'," I chuckle right along with her. I pull out two clean towels and hang them on the fancy towel rack. I flip the switch on the end of it to turn the heater element on. It was already installed in the house when I bought it. Never really thought I'd use it but might as well now that I have a woman in here to impress and take care of.

I step under the water to check the temperature. It is perfect, so I tug Raven into the shower, maneuvering her right under the rainfall shower head she mentioned wanting to try out.

"I think I've died and gone to heaven," she moans as the water cascades down her body. One that is turning me right back on, even after I emptied every last drop inside of her body already tonight, twice.

CHAPTER 16
RAVEN

I STAND JUST OUTSIDE THE SECURITY EXIT, WAITING FOR Tess to come out. Her flight landed ten minutes ago and I'm like a kid in a candy store, excited to see my best friend.

I finally get a glimpse of her as she comes walking down the hall. She is stuck behind a group of people who I swear are walking as slow as a group of sloths. It probably isn't that bad but it sure feels like it.

Tess wraps her arms around me once she reaches me and I embrace her right back.

"I missed you so much," she exclaims. "And look at this cute bump! You are just glowing."

"Thank you. I feel great," I tell her. "Did you check a bag?" I ask.

"Nope, I successfully fit everything in my carryon." She points down to the small suitcase at our feet.

"Let's get out of here then."

"Lead the way." She drapes an arm around my

shoulders as we walk out of the airport and to my car. Even though we talk on a regular basis, if not on the phone, at least by text daily, we still have so much to fill our time with as I drive us back to my place.

"So, how was staying with Mr. Hot Stuff?" she asks once were both changed into some lounge clothes and kicking back with half eaten to-go containers littering my coffee table.

"Is that what you're going to call him?" My head falls back as I laugh at her newest nickname for Blake.

"Hey, if the shoe fits." She shrugs her shoulders.

"It was," I pause, trying to find the right words to describe our time together earlier this week. "Perfect," I finally tell her.

"Eek!" She claps her hands excitedly. "I have a good feeling about this. I really think he's your forever and I hope I'm right," Tess says.

"It's so strange. I feel so comfortable with him and like we've known each other forever. But then I'll think of something and realize I don't know some random fact about him that a long-time friend would know."

"It will come with time. I'm just glad that the two of you aren't going to ignore the obvious connection you have."

"You should have seen him at the baby store." I sigh, remembering just what he looked like holding up some of the newborn baby clothes and how tiny they looked compared to him. "It was quite dreamy, and I swear if I hadn't already been knocked up, I would have been after that visit with him."

"Not sure if you weren't already knocked up by him, the two of you would have been in a baby store together." Tess quirks an eyebrow at me.

"Yeah, yeah. Why do you have to talk logically?" I tease.

"Someone has to stay sane around here," she teases right back. "Speaking of the baby, how's the little gumdrop doing? Have you felt him or her move yet?"

"I had some interesting feelings this morning that I think might have been from the baby, but I also don't know exactly what to expect."

"How was their game last night?" Tess asks.

"They lost, three to two. Blake wasn't in net, but he still feels the loss all the same."

"That must be a strange feeling. Being the one player on the bench that doesn't necessarily play but has to be ready to at any moment."

"I asked him about that, and he says it's all he knows, so to him it isn't strange. Life of being a goalie, I suppose."

"I can see that. They play again tomorrow, correct?" Tess asks.

"Yes, in Buffalo, so the game will be early here thanks to the time difference. It should start around four our time."

"We can plan to watch it, if you'd like," she offers.

I shrug my shoulders. "If we aren't busy. I don't want to have to plan our day around it. It's okay if I don't watch all of the games."

"Did you still want to go decorate your office while I'm here?"

"Yes! I need some cute things to spruce it up."

"I bet we can find some great stuff at Crate and Barrel or Home Goods."

"Sounds like we've got our first two places lined up to stop at tomorrow," I state. "How about we go out for breakfast, then we can go shopping and see where the day takes us?"

"Perfect!" she agrees.

We talk and laugh, paying no attention to the movie that we turned on. I check my phone when she answers a call from Jeremy and see that I have a text from Blake.

Hope your evening with Tess is going well. I just wanted to say good night. Trying to get a good night's sleep in so I'm ready for the game tomorrow. I should be in net.

I don't want to wake him up, so I don't reply. I make a mental note to reply in the morning.

THE WEEKEND FLEW BY WAY TOO QUICKLY. I'M SO thankful that Tess was able to come see me, and it helped pass the time while Blake was gone. We had so much fun shopping and decorating my office, going out for breakfast, walking around the mall, and stopping in every store that sold baby clothes. I swear she's going to buy just as much for this baby as I am. I can't wait to find out if it's a little girl or boy so we know what section we can buy from.

By the time I'm off work tomorrow, he'll be home and waiting for me. The thought of falling asleep in his arms tomorrow night has me drifting into a dream filled sleep, thinking of all the things he'll do to my body once we're back together.

CHAPTER 17
BLAKE

I STEP OFF THE TEAM JET, MY BODY MORE THAN READY TO sleep in my own bed. I played two of the three games, winning both that I was in net for. Not even two hours after the final buzzer sounded last night, we were boarding the team jet to fly back across the country.

Like all the other guys, I quietly gather my suitcases and head to my car. It's just after five in the morning, so a few hours of sleep will do me good. Thankfully, Coach has given us the day off, so I don't have any time commitments other than being ready for Raven when she gets off work this evening.

I make it home, and instantly miss her in my space. When I left on Wednesday, she also was leaving for work. I got used to us having breakfast together those two mornings and having her come home to me at night, where I got to take care of her. It's almost scary how easily we both slipped into this relationship.

I strip out of my travel clothes and drop into bed.

Before I check that I've got an alarm set for noon, I send her a quick text.

> Made it home. Can't wait to see you tonight. Decide what we're having for dinner, and I'll have it ready when you get here. Or do I need to come to you? Let me know. I'm crashing for a few hours, so if I don't respond right away that's why.

I hit the do not disturb setting and make sure my alarm is set for noon, then close my eyes and drift off to thoughts of Raven.

> You know those brownies you bought last week.

> yes… what about them?

> Think you could have some more of them waiting for me? I've been craving them all day.

> Say no more. Any other cravings I should be aware of?

> I'm still on my peanut butter waffle before bed, so some eggs and creamy PB. Please and thank you.

> I thought pregnancy cravings were supposed to be weird combinations like pickles and ice cream?

{shrugging emoji} I'm sure I'll get there at some point.

And I'll be ready to get whatever it is you're craving. {Winking emoji}

You're the best! {Kissy face}

I *think* I felt the baby move today.

Really?! When? Tell me all about it.

Just after I had breakfast, I felt this pressure, almost like an arm rolling along my stomach, just from the inside instead of the outside. It happened so fast but stopped me in my tracks.

So cool. I can't wait until I can feel them move.

Same.

What time do you think you'll get out of work today?

I should be out of here by four-thirty.

Have you decided what you want for dinner, or am I only feeding your brownies?

Do you have any stir fry specialties up your sleeves?

Yes……

Perfect.

> On it.

> See you soon, handsome. {winky face, kissy face}

I DON'T WASTE ANY TIME GRABBING MY KEYS AND HEADING for the grocery store. I stock up on all the items Raven asked for, along with everything I need to make us some stir fry, fried rice, and some crab rangoons for dinner.

"Honey, I'm home," Raven calls out as the door from the garage opens. Before I left last week, I programmed one of the garage door buttons in her car to open my garage. I kind of like having her feel like this house is her home. I can picture us here, kids running around our feet as we dance in the kitchen while cooking dinner together.

"In the kitchen," I call out as I sauté the stir fry.

"Now that is something a girl could get used to," she muses from the doorway.

"Get over here and kiss me, woman," I tell her as I put down the spoon and stalk her way. I wrap her in my arms, dipping her back as my lips find hers. Raven's hands go to my chest, grabbing onto my shirt as my tongue slips past her lips and tangles with hers. The timer on the air fryer going off pulls us apart as I need to swap out the batch of rangoons.

"Duty calls," I say as I right both of us. I hold onto Raven's shoulders for a few extra seconds to make sure she's got her bearings after I just kissed the breath right out of her lungs.

"Can I help with anything?" she breathily asks, her fingers pressing against her kiss swollen lips.

"Sure, you can dump what's in the air fryer out and put in the next batch for four minutes."

Raven gets to work while I move back to the stove. The last batch is coming out of the fryer as I'm removing everything from the stovetop and taking it over to the table, where I've already got plates and silverware set out for the two of us.

"Raspberry lemonade?" I ask Raven.

"Yes, please," she says, and I fill two glasses and bring them to the table.

We sit next to one another, eating and talking, catching up after my trip. We texted and talked most days, but being back together makes a world of a difference.

"Give me your hand," Raven drops her fork and reaches for my hand. I immediately drop my fork and place my hand in hers. She turns it over and presses my palm against her stomach, then just looks at me with a huge smile on her face. "Can you feel that?" she asks, and I can see the hope in her eyes.

"Can you explain what you're feeling?" I ask, hoping I can feel what she does.

"It's like a tapping sensation, right round here," she says, moving my hand for a second so she can draw a circle around the area. She replaces my hand and I press it a little harder against her skin. "There, again." Her face lights up as she must be feeling it stronger now.

I press ever so slightly harder and just then, I feel the

slightest movement against my palm. "There!" I exclaim and can feel tears prick my eyes as I sit here and revel in this moment of getting to feel my unborn child move for the first time. "Thank you." I grip the back of Raven's neck and pull her to me. I kiss her, all while my hand stays glued to her stomach where the baby is moving.

"I think Gumdrop likes it when I eat," Raven says when we break apart.

"I guess so," I agree, a love-struck grin filling my face. I'm already so in love with this baby. I can't even describe the feeling, but he or she isn't the only one I realize I'm in love with.

CHAPTER 18
RAVEN

Blake takes my hand, linking our fingers together as we walk up the pathway to an enormous mansion in front of us. I've been to some nice places, but this place is like nothing I've ever seen before I'm my life. It must be nice to be a tech billionaire who also owns a hockey team.

"Everyone is going to love you," Blake reassures me just before we reach the door that swings open before he can even knock or ring the bell.

"Welcome." We're greeted by a gentleman dressed like a server or butler maybe. Do people still have those? "The party is inside or out on the back patio. Please make yourselves at home," the man instructs.

We make our way down the hall, following the chatter and laughter we can hear coming from those already here. When the room opens up, it is filled with so many people already. I can see kids out the large windows running after one another, a few others jumping into what looks like a huge pool, and more adults than I can count.

Blake tugs me close to his side and walks deeper into the room. "You finally made it," Camden says as he walks up to us.

"We did," I confirm. "I was having a moment and needed to go back to my apartment to find something else to wear. My shorts wouldn't button without cutting off my circulation." Camden's eyes rake down my body and a small smile tugs at his lips.

"When do we find out if I'm having a niece or nephew?" He presses his palm to my stomach, and it makes me melt just a little bit. He's such a softy and is going to be the best uncle to this little gumdrop.

"A few more weeks or so," I tell him. "That is if we decide to find out and then tell you." I smirk at my brother.

"Don't you want to find out?" Blake asks me.

"Definitely, but that doesn't mean I can't hold that information over my brother's head," I tell him as my bother scoffs from beside me.

"Savage," Blake chuckles. "I love it."

"You wouldn't," Camden says. "I'd get Mom to spill the beans."

"What if I don't even tell her?" I ask.

"Like you could keep that information from her?" he says, and I know he's right.

"Sorry to interrupt, but are you Raven?" a pretty blonde asks. She's got a baby on her hip, who's just the cutest.

"I am," I confirm, smiling back at her.

"Perfect. I'm Avery. My husband is Ryker, the team captain," she greets, offering her free hand for me to shake. "I've heard about you and was excited to hear that you'd be attending today. The ladies are all excited to meet you as well. We'd love to have you join us for games and girls' night if that interests you," she rambles on.

"Give the poor girl a minute before you suck her in and not let her go," another woman says as she stops next to Avery. "Hi, I'm Tori. I'm also married to one of the guys. This one can be a little bit overwhelming sometimes, but I'm allowed to call her out on it because we've been friends forever. If it wasn't for her falling in love with her husband, I wouldn't have ever met mine, so I guess I owe her for that," she chuckles.

"Nice to meet you both. Thank you for the invites. I'll probably take you up on them when I'm able to go. I left my best friend back in Anaheim. I really only know these two." I motion to Blake and Camden.

"Oh, honey, we need to get you out for a girls' day for sure. Maybe next weekend when they are on their road trip?" Tori suggests.

"I'm actually busy next weekend," I say and can feel Blake tense next to me.

"What are you doing?" he asks.

"I'm going down to Anaheim for the weekend," I tell him, "It's my best friend, Tess's, birthday weekend, and her husband is throwing her a surprise party. She has no idea I'm coming down for it," I explain to Tori.

"Sounds like a fun weekend!" Tori says.

"I couldn't pass up going down when Jeremy called me," I tell them.

"Of course. Go have fun and we can include you in the next time we all get together. Before you leave today, let's exchange numbers and we can be in touch as the week goes by. Once we have an idea of what our next get together will be, I'll loop you in on the plans," Tori suggests.

"That sounds perfect," I tell her.

"Can we steal you away for a couple of minutes and introduce you to the others?" Avery asks.

I look at Blake, and he just shrugs but brings his lips to my ear. "They're going to love you," he reminds me.

"I guess so," I answer. Avery practically squeals in excitement as she reaches for my arm. She tugs me behind her to the laugher of Blake, Camden and Tori, who keeps up with both of us. She leads me to a group of women, all of whom are standing around chatting amongst themselves. "Ladies," Avery interrupts the group, and they all turn their attention her way. "I have someone new to introduce," she says. "This is Raven. She is Camden's sister and Blake's girlfriend," she tells everyone, then turns to me. "Oh crap, you two are dating, yes?" she asks, realizing that she might have just assumed that part.

I let her sweat it out for a few seconds before letting her off the hook. "Yes, we're dating and having a baby together," I say just to get that out in the open.

"Congratulations, when are you due?" one of the women asks.

"Middle of April," I tell them.

"Perfect time to have a baby. Playoff time," someone else says.

"All right, I'll quickly tell you who everyone is, and who they are connected with, but we don't expect you to remember any of it. So don't feel bad if you need to ask us who is who later," Avery says as we all stand in a circle. "Tori is married to Aiden. Next to her is Trinity. She's with Damien, but she also works for the team as the social media manager. They met at work and fell in love," Avery explains. "Then we have Kendra. she's married to Tristan."

"It is so nice to meet all of you," I tell them sincerely.

"I know it can be a bit overwhelming at first, but I promise you this is the best group of ladies to be pulled in by," Kendra tells me. "They were my lifeline when I first came to live with Tristan. I'd be so lost without them."

"Thanks. I will admit, moving away from my best friend wasn't easy, but I have a feeling that I'll do just fine here amongst all of you."

"We have a group chat we can add you to. If you need anything, you summon the ladies," Trinity says.

"Exactly," Tori reiterates. "Especially the further into your pregnancy you get. If the guys are on the road, we'll be there for whatever it is you need."

"Thank you," I tell them all and have to hold back tears at their kindness. I never dreamed my life would turn out like this when I saw those two pink lines on one test and pregnant on the other.

"Are you ladies done with my girl here, or can I steal her away?" Blake asks.

"Who knew you were such a teddy bear?" Avery asks Blake.

"All you had to do was ask." He smirks. "That and put the right woman in front of me." He wraps a hand around my back, resting it on my opposite hip. He escorts me over to a large buffet table, covered in just about any kind of food someone might want to eat.

We both fill our plates with a mixture of all the amazing dishes that are set out. This was definitely catered by the looks of all there is to choose from. I make my way over to a large grazing table. It is one long charcuterie board, which is my kryptonite. All I'm missing is a good glass of wine, which I can't have again until this little one makes an appearance.

"Hello, I'm Harper," a friendly woman greets me when I make it to the end of the table.

"Hi, I'm Raven," I reply.

"Who are you here with?" she asks.

"Blake, but Camden is also my brother," I explain.

"It's nice to meet you. Welcome to our home, we're happy to have you with us today. Nathan and I enjoy hosting the team and their families at the beginning of every season."

"Your home is gorgeous," I complement Harper.

"Thank you. I'm quite fond of this place. It took

forever to design and wait for it to be built, but I love it."

"Did you design all of it?" I ask. While I haven't seen very much of it, what I have seen is impressive.

"With the help of some amazing designers, yes. I had ideas in mind from looking at endless listings and compiled all my favorite things from everywhere and came up with this place."

"That must have been fun."

"Most of the time," she laughs lightly, "except for the moments I was ready to pull my hair out because things weren't going to plan."

"Well, from what I've seen, it is perfect." One of the servers pulls Harper away, so I head over to find an open seat next to Blake. He's sitting with a few of the other guys, but he stops to stand and pull out the chair next to him so I can sit down.

"You good, darlin'?" he whispers in my ear after I sit down, and he helps slide my chair closer to the table.

A shiver runs through my body thanks to his breath on my neck. "Yes," I say as I nod.

We eat and visit with almost everyone here. Blake was right that I'd feel at home with this group of people. The girls all pull me right in and I'm happy to have met all of them as I definitely need some girl-friends in my new city.

CHAPTER 19
BLAKE

THE LAST FEW WEEKS HAVE PRACTICALLY FLOWN BY. I'M well into the hockey season, we're gelling as a team and on course to have our best season yet as the newest team in the league.

The day has finally arrived for Raven's ultrasound where we get to find out the baby's gender. I'm stoked to know if I'll have a son or daughter after today. We're having a gender reveal party this weekend when our parents are all coming to town.

"How are you doing, Momma?" I ask Raven as I rub her belly as she lays next to me in bed.

"Excited. Nervous. I have so many emotions running through me right now, I don't know what one takes precedence ," she chuckles.

"Your gut still telling you it's a girl?" I ask. She's been saying that for the last couple of weeks after a dream she had. She said in the dream she could see me pushing a little girl with pigtails on a swing. Ever since she described it to me, I haven't been able to get rid of that image.

"Yes, and I was thinking of the name Abigail. Call her Abby for short."

"Abby," I roll the name around in my head and tongue. "I like it. Abigail. Any ideas or a middle name?" I ask.

"Nothing came to mind right away, so I Googled it. One suggestion I liked was Brynn," Raven says. "Abigail Brynn Watson. It flows nicely."

"You're going to give her my last name?" I whisper my question, the emotion hitting me. We haven't discussed it yet, but I've had thoughts about it.

Raven rolls to face me, cupping my cheek once she's settled on her side. I cup hers, rubbing my thumb across her cheek.

"Why wouldn't we? She should have her dad's last name."

"Thank you. Hopefully one day, you'll have it as well." I lean in and kiss her before she can reply. It is way too soon to be discussing marriage, but I know deep down that is where we'll end up one day. It might not be this year, but one day I'll make this woman my wife.

The alarm Raven set on her phone rings, startling both of us and making us pull apart. "Time to get ready so we're not late."

We both roll out of bed. "I'll go make some breakfast while you shower."

"You're so good to me." She stops to give me a quick kiss before heading into the bathroom. I'm hopeful I can convince her to just move into my house when her lease ends in a few months. Hell, I'll buy her out if it is needed. She's here almost every night that I'm home, and I like the idea of her being here when I'm on the road. Plus, here in the next few weeks, we need to start working on the nursery, and focusing on just one seems like a better idea than two.

I head for the kitchen and pull out some pre-chopped veggies, diced ham, and cheese to make a scrambled egg mixture. I heat up a couple tortillas before filling them with the eggs . I top them off with some salsa and finish wrapping them up as breakfast burritos.

"Something smells amazing," Raven says as she enters the kitchen. She's in a pair of maternity jeans and a flowy top that shows off her cute belly.

"Breakfast burritos," I tell her as she pours herself a glass of orange juice.

"Thank you." She stops to give me a chaste kiss.

"Eat up. We've got a baby to go see." I wink, then dive into my food.

I grab a quick shower, then we're on the road to her doctor's office.

"Raven," a nurse calls from the doorway between the waiting room and the back area.

We both stand and with my hand on her lower back, we walk toward the lady standing in the doorway.

"Good morning, I'm Dawn. I'll be performing your

ultrasound today," she explains as she leads us to the exam room. "Go ahead and lie down on the table. I'll have to push your pants down, then I'll tuck this towel into them just to keep the gel from making a mess on them. If any time you are uncomfortable, just let me know."

"Okay," Raven says as she gets settled on the table and lowers her jeans down. Dawn tucks the towel in and then squirts some gel onto her stomach.

"Ready?" Dawn asks as she presses the ultrasound probe against Raven's belly.

"Absolutely, and we'd like to know the gender, please," Raven tells her.

I grab her hand, linking our fingers together as we both look up at the large TV screen hanging on the wall. Our baby fills the screen, and I'm enamored with how clearly I can make things out.

"I'm just checking baby's skull size. Everything looks good with that," Dawn explained as she presses all sorts of buttons on her machine. "Next is the heart," she says as she presses another button, and the room is filled with the sound of a beating heart.

"Is that the baby's?" I ask.

"It is," Dawn confirms.

Tears spring to my eyes as I take in this experience. I'm so fucking thankful for that night in Vegas and then for Raven coming to that first game.

"All right, now the moment you've both been waiting for," Dawn says as she moves the probe. The baby moves as she pushes in a new spot on Raven's belly. "Little stinker rolled away from me." Dawn chuckles as she readjusts. "Okay, so any final guesses?" she asks us.

"I still think girl," Raven tells her.

"I'm going to go with Mom here," I say.

"I'm happy to confirm your suspicions. You're having a baby girl!" Dawn confirms.

"Abigail," I say, finally having a name for our baby. I lean in and kiss Raven. "I hope she looks just like you," I whisper against her lips before pulling back.

Dawn takes a few more measurements, before printing out a long strip of pictures that she hands to me. "Everything looks great. The doctor will take a look at these when you see him shortly. You can go ahead and wipe off your stomach and when you're ready, I can show you down to the exam room."

"Thank you," Raven says as she wipes off her stomach with the towels Dawn provides.

She escorts us down a hall. "You can take a seat in room four," Dawn tells me. "And you can use the bathroom. There should be a collection cup in there for you."

"Thanks," I say as I dip into the room and take a seat on one of the chairs in the corner.

Raven joins me a few minutes later, a nurse following her into the room. "How are you feeling lately?" she asks her as Raven takes a seat at the end of the exam table.

"Really good. My energy has returned. I'm feeling baby girl daily now, and just really enjoying this part of my pregnancy."

"That's great to hear!" she says as she types on her tablet. "Any bouts of morning sickness still happening?"

"Nope, I'm over those thankfully."

The nurse asks her a few more questions before leaving, letting us know the doctor will be in shortly.

"Can you believe it; we're having a little girl!" Raven smiles at me and I can see just how happy she is.

"She already owns my heart, kind of like her momma does," I say as the door opens and in walks a middle-aged man wearing a white coat.

"Hello, I'm Dr. Mike Davis." He holds a hand out to greet me. This is the first appointment I've been to since I was out of town for Raven's first one since she moved here.

"Blake Watson. Nice to meet you." I give him a firm shake.

"The hockey player?" he asks.

"The one and only," I confirm.

"My son is a big fan; just started playing goalie this year because of you."

"Wow, that's awesome. You'll have to tell him I say good luck. I can send over some tickets and a signed jersey for him if you'd like."

"That's very kind of you," Dr. Davis says as he takes a seat on the stool. "How are you doing today?" He turns his attention to Raven.

"Great. I'm feeling good. Energy is back. Baby is moving." she tells him as she did his nurse.

"Great to hear. The ultrasound images all look great. Baby girl is measuring right on track. I didn't see anything alarming," he explains to the both of us.

"Do you have any questions?"

"I can't think of any," Raven tells him, then looks at me with questioning eyes. I shake my head no, as I don't.

"If you think of anything before your next appointment, don't hesitate to call or send a message through the app. At your next appointment, we'll go ahead and do your gestational diabetes test, which consists of you drinking a special drink, then one hour later, we'll draw your labs and check your glucose levels. You can eat and drink normally before the test. Just avoid sugary things as that can skew your results. Then once you drink the surgery drink, you can only have small amounts of water until after we draw your blood."

"Sounds simple enough."

"It really is, and don't stress about it. Approximately twenty-five percent of women fail the one-hour test. If that happens, then we'll do the three-hour test."

"Sounds good. I was expecting the one-hour at either my next appointment or the one after that based on what I've read in my pregnancy books."

"Standard testing time is between twenty-four and twenty-eight weeks. I like to shoot for the twenty-four-week mark just to have some wiggle room in case schedules don't line up properly."

"Makes sense," Raven says.

"If no other questions, I'll let you get out of here and see you back in a month," he says to Raven, offering his hand for her to shake. "Nice to meet you," Dr. Davis says, offering his hand to me once again.

"Likewise. Should I shoot that package here to your office?" I ask him before he walks out of the room.

"Sure, but please don't feel obligated."

"Not at all," I confirm.

Dr. Davis leaves the room first. I follow Raven up to the checkout desk where she stops to schedule her next appointment. She's able to get a morning appointment on a home game day, so I can still make it to the optional morning skate if I want to that day. Since she has to be here an hour beforehand for her test, they open the lab an hour early for those patients that want to get it done first thing in the morning.

"How about we stop at the store on the way home," I suggest. I have the desire to go buy my daughter some stuff now that we know it's a girl.

"I swear you can read my mind sometimes." Raven smiles at me as we walk hand-in-hand out to the car.

I drive us back to the baby store we went to on our date. This time we head straight for the girl section and before we know it, we have a cart full of pink and purple everything, ranging in size from newborn to twelve months.

"All right, I think we've gone overboard," Raven laughs as she looks at the cart.

"If you say so." I laugh at the pile. "Should we pick

out the crib?" I ask, nodding toward that section of the store.

"We can look, but I also would like to paint her room at your place if you don't mind. I can't at my condo, but figured we could go all out at your house."

I take this opening. Pulling Raven to stand in front of me, I tip her chin up so I can look into her beautiful hazel eyes. "What do you think about just moving in with me? No more going back and forth. You spend most of your time at my house as it is. Why don't we just make it official?" I ask, then hold my breath as I wait for her to answer.

"Are you sure?" she asks.

"I've never been more sure about anything. I love you, Raven. I want everything that comes with building a family together."

The way her face lights up with a full smile has me breathing a sigh of relief. "I'd love nothing more, and I love you, too, Blake."

I drop my lips to hers, but I keep it quick since we are standing in the middle of a baby store.

"When is your lease up?" I ask. "I can buy you out of it, if necessary," I offer.

"I only signed a six-month lease just in case I didn't end up liking the place, so it will end in March."

"My offer stands if you want me to just buy it out. We can get some movers lined up to move everything and just put it in the garage until we decide what to do with it."

"No sense in paying a mover to moving most of the

furniture since your house is fully furnished. I'll just list it online and only bring all my personal things."

"Whatever you want to do, darlin'," I say as we start moving again. We look at the cribs, but don't decide on one today. First up is painting the nursery.

CHAPTER 20
RAVEN
THREE MONTHS LATER

I stand up and walk to the back of the living room, not wanting to block anyone's view of the TV. These Braxton Hicks contractions have been strong today, almost taking my breath away at times, but walking seems to help, or at least it did when I was at work today.

"Everything okay?" Tori asks as she sees me swaying back and forth.

"I think so, just some Braxton Hicks contractions."

"Those were the devil," she sympathizes with me.

"I just started having them, but man, are they strong tonight. I also have had this lingering headache all day that won't go away," I tell her.

"Any other new symptoms?" she asks.

"I got dizzy once, but I think I just stood up to fast."

"Have you had any issues with high blood pressure?" she asks.

"Not that I'm aware of. It's usually pretty normal at all my appointments, why?"

"Some of your symptoms are those they watch for in pre-eclampsia. Are you nauseous? Or have you noticed any unusual swelling?"

Tears prick the back of my eyes as fear starts to set in. "Yeah, my feet were really swollen this morning when I woke up, but I just chalked it up to normal pregnancy symptoms."

"Avery," Tori calls out, motioning for her to come join us. While Avery walks our way, Tori pulls out a chair and points for me to sit down. "Grab a cold, wet washcloth," she instructs Avery.

"Here, is everything okay?" Avery asks when she returns. She presses the cold rag to my forehead, which feels good, but also makes me realize how warm I'm feeling suddenly.

"I'm dizzy and lightheaded."

"I think we need to take you to the hospital to get checked out. Do you think you can walk to my car safely?" Tori asks.

"I think so," I tell her as I try to stand, but the next thing I know my world is dark.

"Raven, can you open your eyes for me? Someone call 911." I hear the words but find it hard to open my eyes.

I finally open them slightly and see Tori and Avery

hovering over me as I lay on the floor. I move my head, but it throbs with every movement. "What happened?" I ask as tears roll down my cheeks.

"You passed out. We've got an ambulance on the way. Just take some deep breaths for me and try to stay calm," Avery says as Tori talks on the phone next to us.

"Can someone open the door?" Tori calls out to the room. I'm guessing one of the other ladies goes to it, opening it for the paramedics as they start to surround me.

"Hi Raven, I'm Marcus. Can you tell me what's going on?"

"I've had a headache all day, and woke up with some swelling. I've had some Braxton Hicks contractions all day, and apparently, I passed out." I tell him. "I'm thirty-four weeks pregnant." I add, my head still pounding.

"I was worried about pre-eclampsia and was trying to get her out to my car to drive her to the hospital when she passed out," Tori explains to the paramedics.

They take my vitals and get me on the stretcher. "Blood pressure is pretty high. I think it's safe to say you've earned yourself a trip to the hospital tonight," Marcus tells me.

"Can you call Blake?" I ask Avery. "And Camden," I add as an afterthought.

"We'll take care of it. You just worry about you and the baby," Avery tells me as they start to wheel me out of the house.

"I'll follow you to the hospital," Tori tells me as they load me into the back of the ambulance.

"Thank you," I say just before they close the doors, and the ambulance pulls away.

"I'd like to get an IV hooked up and some fluids started for you if you're okay with that," Marcus says as he pulls out some supplies from one of the compartments in the ambulance.

"Of course," I say, holding out my arm for him. He checks for a vein and preps my arm. It stings when the needle goes in, but thankfully that doesn't last long.

"You doing okay?" he asks and I notice he's watching a monitor that has my vitals on it.

"Not really. This headache is getting worse, and the dizzy feeling is coming back," I tell him.

"We're almost to the hospital, and they can get you assessed further. I've given you some meds in the IV, so hopefully you'll start to have some relief from both the headache and nausea."

"Thank you," I say as I close my eyes. I can feel the tears falling still. All I can think the rest of the way to the hospital is I wish Blake was here.

It's a whirlwind at the hospital after I'm brought in. The paramedics bypass the ER and take me directly to the triage section of the labor and delivery department. They hook me up to monitors immediately and start assessing my symptoms and give me some additional meds.

Thankfully my headache finally goes away, as does the nausea and the dizzy feeling.

"How are you feeling?" a nurse asks when she comes back into my little area.

"Better," I tell her as I watch as she checks my vitals.

"That's great to hear. We're just waiting for Dr. Davis to respond to his page so we can see what he'd like to do."

"Do you think it's likely I'll be admitted to the hospital?" I ask.

"It's possible, but you responded quickly to the meds, so that's a good sign."

"Do I have pre-eclampsia?" I ask.

"I can't officially diagnose, but yes. Your symptoms were pretty textbook, but I'd say you are on the beginning edge of it, so with meds, it should be controllable."

"Everything has been going so well; I never expected this to happen," I say more to myself than the nurse.

"Things can change in the snap of your fingers. You did nothing wrong to cause this to happen, so don't even go down that road of doubt. Pre-eclampsia can happen at any time during any pregnancy."

"Knock-knock, can I come in?" I hear Tori's voice from the doorway.

"Sure can," the nurse turns her way and gives her a quick smile.

"How are you feeling?" she asks as she stands next to the bed.

"Better," I say.

"Good. I wanted to let you know I got ahold of Trinity. She was going to get word to Coach before talking to Blake and Camden."

"Thanks for taking care of that."

"Of course; we're all one big family. It's what we do;" Tori assures me.

"Your vitals are looking good, so I'm going to let you visit and will be back to check on you. If you need anything before then, don't hesitate to press the call button."

"Will do," I assure her before she leaves the room.

"I'm so worried that Blake is going to flip out when he finds out I'm in the hospital."

"Probably, but just like you've got all of us here to help you, he's got the team to support him."

"Never thought of that," I say. "How much longer until the game ends?"

"It ended a little bit ago, so it wouldn't surprise me if you get a call soon," she says just as my phone starts buzzing in her hand. "Speaking of the devil," she smiles and answers the phone for me. "Hello," she says. "Hey, Blake, this is Tori," she says then pauses. "Yeah, I'm right here with Raven. She's doing much better. Gave us a little scare at the watch party, but I think the doctors have figured out what is going on and are treating her accordingly," she explains. "Yes, just a second," she says and holds the phone out to me.

"Hello," I say, emotion filling my voice as I do.

"Darlin," he croaks. "Please tell me everything is going to be okay."

"It will be. I'm waiting on Dr. Davis to arrive to give me the full details on what's going on and if I have to stay in the hospital or can be sent home."

"If you are sent home, please ask one of the wives to stay with you until I can get home. I don't want you left alone just in case."

"I'll ask," I tell him. Thankfully he's headed home after tonight's game, so he should be home by morning. "How was the game?" I ask, needing something else to focus on.

"Okay, we won in overtime," he says.

"Nice, I didn't make it through the first period," I tell him.

"It's been that long and I'm just now finding out?" he says and I can tell he's irritated about that.

"Tori mentioned she finally reached Trinity, who then had to get the info to Coach, and then finally to you and Camden. I think she was focused on making sure I was taken care of first."

"I appreciate that, but still am irritated it took so long for me to know something happened," he grumbles, and I can understand his frustration.

"Hold on, Dr. Davis is coming in," I tell him.

"Put me on speaker so I can hear what's going on?" Blake asks and I do just that.

"Well, well, I hear you've had an eventful day," Dr. Davis says as he enters the room.

"I guess you could say that," I say. "Blake is on speaker phone; he's just finished a game in Seattle." I explain the reasoning for the phone being on while he's in the room.

"No problem, nice win tonight," Dr. Davis says.

"Thanks, can you explain what's going on?" Blake asks.

"Raven has a condition known as pre-eclampsia. It is treatable, sometimes just by meds and rest. Taking things easy, not over doing it. Other times, it requires full hospital bed rest. Since you passed out, I'd like to err on the side of caution and admit you for at least tonight. I don't want you to get home, the meds wear off and you're right back in the same spot and needing immediate treatment. By keeping you in, we can monitor you closely and adjust your meds as necessary. If everything looks good, we can send you home tomorrow."

"Okay," I agree with his suggestion. I'll always do what is best for both my baby and me, and right now, I feel like staying in the hospital overnight is the best thing for me.

"I like that. I won't be home until the middle of the night, so knowing nurses and doctors will be close by helps calm me slightly," Blake says over the phone.

"I'll get the paperwork started and they'll get you moved into a full room."

"Am I allowed to eat anything?" I ask. "I haven't eaten much today due to the nausea but am feeling hungry now."

"Yes, I'm not sure what the nurses can get you right

now, but I'll put in an order for a tray. Or anyone can bring you food as well if you prefer," he says.

"I can go grab you anything," Tori pipes up. "Just let me know and I'll make it happen."

"I'm going to go grab a shower and get on the bus. Call or text if anything changes. I'll come straight to the hospital when we land, so text me your hospital room once you have it. Okay, darlin'?"

"Okay, I love you," I tell him.

"I love you, too, both of you," he says before the call disconnects.

It doesn't take long before I'm being moved to a hospital room and being fully admitted for the night. I'm exhausted by the time they get me settled, but thankfully Tori returns about that time with some soup and a half of a sandwich for me to eat. It might be fast food, but at least it is something at this point. I was ready to chew my dang arm off I was getting so hungry.

"Feel better?" she asks once I've finished devouring my food.

"So much. Thank you again for everything. I didn't mean to mess up everyone's night. Speaking of, where is Carter?" I ask about her son.

"Avery kept him for me. He had the night of his life getting to stay up late and play. He's doing perfectly fine being spoiled," she says.

"If you need to go to him, you can. I'm safe now that I'm being monitored."

"He's perfectly fine where he is. You, on the other

hand, need someone by your side, and tonight that is me. Unless you truly don't want me here, I don't plan on going anywhere."

Tori's kindness hits me hard. I know I just need to accept it, and I know deep down that any of the women at the watch party would drop everything to help one another, and now I'm lucky enough to be part of that exclusive club of wives and girlfriends of the players.

"Thank you, and please pass on my thanks to everyone else. I'm sorry I messed up such a good night."

"You didn't mess up anything. The safety of you and the baby are more important than any of us watching a hockey game."

"I just hate making a scene, and well, passing out and needing an ambulance to come rescue me, definitely made a scene."

"It wasn't that bad, I promise. Some kept the kids there occupied while the paramedics worked on you and got you out of there. Others stayed after to help clean up. All is good, I promise."

"If you say so, I'll believe you."

We visit for a little longer, but I'm exhausted. I've had a big day and I'm ready to try to get some sleep.

With Tori's help, I shift around, getting comfortable on my left side. I'm finally able to doze off and get a little sleep for the next few hours.

I wake up to the feeling of a large, warm hand holding my own. My eyes slowly open and immediately find Blake's. He's standing at the edge of my hospital bed, dark circles under each eye and his hair going every which way, like he's been running his hands through it since we talked on the phone last night.

"Hi," I say just above a whisper.

"Hey, darlin'," he says as he lowers down to kiss me. "How are my girls doing this morning?"

"Much better," I tell him. It's then I notice my brother is also standing in my room. He's leaning against the wall near the door, taking in everything. "Hi, Camden."

"Hey, sis. Gave us quite the scare last night. Glad you're feeling better today."

"Yeah, it was quite the evening. Not my finest moments, that's for sure," I tell him.

"Do we know yet if they're going to let you come home today?" Blake asks.

"No idea. I don't think the doctor has come in yet this morning. What time is it anyway?" I ask.

"Just after seven-thirty," Blake says.

"How long have the two of you been here?"

"A few hours; came straight from the airport. You were sleeping so peacefully I didn't want to wake you, so I've just been sitting here next to your bed. I sent Tori home, told her to get some sleep and we'd call with an update once we had one."

"You look tired," I say, reaching up to cup his cheek. I rub the dark circle under one of his eyes.

"I'll be fine. I needed to see you with my own eyes. Know for sure that you were going to be okay."

"Good morning," a cheerful voice rings into the room. "Hello, I'm Heidi. I'm one of the day nurses."

"Hello, nice to meet you."

"I just wanted to check in and see how you're feeling and introduce myself. Breakfast should be delivered soon if you're hungry."

"I am pretty hungry; do you know when Dr. Davis should be here?" I ask.

"He usually does rounds over the next hour, so I imagine it won't be long," she explains.

"Perfect, I'm hoping I get to go home today."

"You should know that once he stops in to see you."

"Perfect. While you're in here, do you mind unhooking my IV so I can use the restroom?"

"Not at all," Heidi says as she presses some buttons on the IV stand. She then disconnects the lines and helps me out of bed. Thankfully my room has its own private bathroom, so I don't have far to go.

I get myself settled back into bed and Heidi reconnects my IV line before leaving the room, promising to return when the doctor arrives.

"Did you want me to run to your place and pick anything up?" Camden offers.

"Maybe, but I can wait until after talking to the doctor. If he's going to discharge me, then there isn't any need. I can just get anything once I'm home."

"Fair enough," Camden says as he sits in one of the visitor chairs.

"You don't have to stay. Why don't you go home and get some sleep?" I suggest.

"I'll be fine, it shouldn't be long until the doctor is here," he says.

We're interrupted by an employee bringing in a breakfast tray. I don't care that it is bland hospital food. I'm starving, so I dig right into the scrambled eggs, toast, ham, and hash browns. Just as I'm finishing up, Dr. Davis comes in, Heidi just behind him.

"Good morning, Raven," he greets, offering his hand for me to shake.

"Morning, Doc," I greet him back. "Are you here to give me good news that I'm being sent home?" I ask hopeful.

"I am, your vitals looked good throughout the night. But there's a catch to being sent home," he says, and I don't care what the stipulations are, I'll follow them to a T. "You'll be on a low dose blood pressure medication. I want you on modified bed rest. Meaning you can move about your house, but no going out and walking around Target or the mall. If you need to go, then use one of the motorized carts. I want you to get an at home blood pressure machine and check yours three times a day. I also want to see you in my office in two days for a follow-up. No work. I'll give you a doctor's note for medical leave and fill out any FMLA paperwork you need me to fill out. If any symptom comes back, no matter how small, you come straight back to the hospital."

"Not a problem at all." I assure him. "Am I allowed to drive?"

"I'd prefer you have someone to drive you, but if

that isn't feasible and you have no other options, then you may."

"Should we have someone with her at all times?" Blake asks the doctor.

"It wouldn't be a bad idea," Dr. Davis says.

"I'm sure we can make arrangements. Tori has already texted me saying all the ladies are more than willing to step in and help in any way we need," Blake tells me.

"I don't want to be a burden to anyone," I tell him.

"You aren't a burden to anyone," he says, cutting that idea off.

"I'll get the orders in for your meds, and the discharge process started. Expect a call from my office in the next hour to schedule that appointment for in two days," Dr. Davis says. "If you don't have any further questions, I'll get out of your hair so we can get you on your way home."

"Thank you," Blake says to the doctor as they shake hands.

"Unless you need me to stick around, I'm going to head home and get some sleep. How about I bring some dinner over tonight?" Camden offers.

"Sounds good, man. Thanks for sticking around with me," Blake says as they do the man hand-slap, hug bit. I love seeing how their friendship has deepened in the last few months.

"See you later, sis," Camden says as he leans down to give me a hug and kiss on my cheek.

"Thanks again for coming," I give him an extra squeeze before letting him go.

"Anytime. Text me later with what you want for dinner," he says before leaving my hotel room.

Blake finally takes a seat, but not before pulling the chair over so he's close enough to hold my hand. "How's our little girl doing?" Blake asks as he rubs my belly.

"Perfectly fine. Using my bladder as a trampoline still," I chuckle. She must hear her daddy's voice as she starts kicking his hand.

"Baby girl, we've had this conversation before. You need to be kind to your mother. She's doing her best to bring you into this world healthy." I tear up at his words to our daughter. I can't wait to see her in his arms. I'm sure my ovaries will explode at the sight. The way he is with her now and she isn't even born yet is mind blowing.

"Good news," Heidi says as she pushes into the room. "I come bearing your discharge paperwork and am going to spring you free."

"Perfect," I say as she pulls out some supplies from a cart in the room.

"Let's get this IV out of your arm first," she says as she starts removing the tape that holds it in place. It doesn't take long before she's wrapping a bandage around my arm and just like that, I'm no longer hooked up to the tubes. She goes over the discharge instructions once again, then brings me the bag with the clothes I had on last night so I can change back into them from the hospital gown they had me put on.

"Good luck, and I hope we don't see you back until it's time to deliver that precious little one," she says as Blake helps me up and into the waiting wheelchair they've called to take me down to the car. I guess this is something I've got to get used to for the next few weeks.

Blake drives us straight home. He doesn't want me to have to wait in the car any longer than necessary, so home it is.

"Where do you want to relax? Living room or bedroom?"

"The couch for now, unless you want to take a nap with me?" I ask.

"I definitely won't pass up that offer," he says. "But before I lie down, I'm going to go grab your meds and anything else you want from the store."

"Okay," I say. "Can you grab me a strawberry refresher from Starbucks?" I bat my eyelashes at him.

"Anything for you, darlin'." He presses his lips to mine but doesn't push it deeper. "Do you want any specific snacks?"

"Can you grab a couple freezer meals that I can just pop in the microwave or oven? Like the single lasagna, mac and cheese, maybe a potpie one."

"Of course. Do you want any fruits or veggies?"

"Grapes, maybe some strawberries if they have them. I think we still have some veggies in the fridge I can snack on," I tell him. "And if we don't, I can do a grocery delivery order."

"Okay, I'll be back as quickly as I can." He kisses me before heading out. I head to our bedroom; I need a shower and some clean clothes before I lie down.

I take it easy since I'm home alone. Last night was scary, so I'm thankful I was with the girls when I passed out. I'd hate to think what could have happened had I been home alone.

CHAPTER 21
BLAKE

I SWEAR FROM THE MOMENT COACH CALLED ME AND Camden aside as soon as the game ended last night my heart rate increased and raced until I was standing in the hospital room and the doctor told us that Raven could go home. I've never been so nervous or scared in my life.

I head up to the pharmacy counter. "How can I help you?" the employee asks.

"I'm here to pick up some prescriptions for Raven Rowe," I tell him.

"Looks like we've got two new ones for her. Can you confirm her date of birth please."

"July twenty-second," I answer and he steps away to pull the meds from the waiting bins.

"Total is fourteen dollars and seventy-three cents."

I swipe my credit card, then step to the next window as the pharmacist has to go over the meds with me since they are new. Thankfully it is quick and

I'm out the door and across the parking lot where a Super Target is located. I grab the food Raven requested, load up on the fruit, and even hit up the Starbucks counter before I head back to my car. I'm pretty proud of myself for accomplishing everything in less than a half hour.

I make it home and am a little worried when I come inside and it is silent. My stomach drops that something has happened. "Raven," I call out, listening for her to reply. When I hear nothing, I drop the groceries and go running for the bedroom. It's then that I hear the water running in the bathroom. "Darlin', you in here?" I call out as I open the door.

"Yeah, you're back already?" she asks.

"That I am. I didn't want to leave you for too long," I say.

"I've just been relaxing with the water on me and kind of lost track of time, I guess," she says, poking her pretty face out of the curtain.

"I got worried when it was silent in the house when I returned. I'll let you finish up while I go put every-thing away. Do you want anything to eat right now?"

"Maybe just a bowl of fruit. Did you get my drink?" she asks.

"I did. It's downstairs. Do you want me to bring your snack and drink up here?"

"Are you lying down to nap?" she asks.

"Probably. I need some sleep soon."

"Then yes, bring it up. I'll lie down with you. I'm kind of tired."

"I'll be back shortly," I tell her before heading back down.

I hand over a cereal size bowl, filled half with grapes and half with sliced strawberries. "Thank you," Raven says.

"Anything for you, darlin'."

I can't hold back my yawn. I'm starting to feel the impact of playing an NHL game last night, followed by not sleeping a wink since my pre-game nap yesterday.

"Lie down and go to sleep," Raven says, patting my side of the bed. I don't have to be told twice, so I strip down to my boxer briefs and slide between the sheets. I curl on my side, facing Raven, and snake my hand out to place it on her belly. I've been doing this for months now and it has become one of my favorite things. Abby usually will wake up and kick back, almost like she's giving me hi-fives.

"Love you both," I say before sleep claims me.

SHOCKWAVES

WE MAKE IT TWO WEEKS WITH RAVEN ON BED REST AT home before her blood pressure spikes again and she's back in the hospital. Thankfully this time, I wasn't at an away game when it happened.

"I think you're going to be in here until this baby is born," Dr. Davis explains to both of us. "We're going to do everything we can to make that a few more weeks down the road, but if not, you're in the best possible place. We've got one of the best NICU departments that will assess the baby as soon as she's born and take any necessary steps to make sure she's healthy when it's time for you to take her home."

"What can we expect over the next few weeks?" I ask.

"We're going to give a shot of a steroid to help the baby's lungs in case she was to come early. For the next week, we will do everything we can to keep you pregnant; once you hit thirty-seven weeks, we won't stop labor if you were to go into it. We will evaluate your blood pressure and other symptoms if it happens before then and make a game time decision," Dr. Davis explains. "No matter when it happens, we'll be ready and prepared." He assures us both.

"Am I allowed to move around much?" Raven asks.

"You can for sure get up to shower, use the restroom; small tasks like that. I'll put approval in your chart that you can walk around the unit halls twice a day as long as your blood pressure is within normal range. If the nurses see anything that doesn't look right, they'll let you know it isn't safe and that you need to stay on bed rest."

"Okay," she agrees to his orders.

Once Dr. Davis has left the two of us alone, the emotions hits Raven.

"Come here," I say, opening my arms wide. She steps into my embrace and melts into me. I wrap my arms around her, holding her tight to me. "I've got you, babe," I whisper into her ear. Her body shakes as she sobs into my chest and it fucking breaks my heart.

"Why can't my body just be normal and keep both me and our baby safe until she's born?" she asks, and I know she's just frustrated with the situation.

"Hey, your body is amazing. Yes, we've had some setbacks, but you are still growing an entire human. Don't be so hard on yourself. It is having to work over-time to grow a tiny person. Take the next day, week or month and try to relax. I know that is easier said than done, but the better you get at relaxing, the longer your body will be able to keep her inside and getting bigger."

"I don't know how I would have done all of this without you," she says, looking up at me.

"And you never will." I drop a kiss to her lips as a nurse comes into the room.

"Good to see you again, although I'd hoped it would have been when you were in labor," the nurse, Heidi, who discharged us a few weeks ago, says as she comes into the room. "I need to get your IV started so we can get your meds going. Do you have a preference on what arm I use?" she asks.

"Hello, again," Raven greets. "I'm not super picky. Can you try for my forearm though, so it isn't in the way? I hate when they're put into my hand or the bend of my arm."

"Absolutely. I prefer them there as well. Easier to still have use of your arm."

I help get Raven settled into the hospital bed. Heidi points out a cabinet that is stocked with extra pillows and blankets. "Feel free to use as many of those as necessary to make Raven comfortable. You can also bring things from home. Just don't bring anything you wouldn't want fluids accidentally getting on if her water was to break."

"Noted," I say, already starting a mental list of things I'll need to bring her. We got sent here from one of her biweekly checkups, so she doesn't even have a charger for her phone.

"Bring her some comfortable lounge clothes. We don't require our moms to be that are on bed rest to be in hospital gowns. Shower stuff, your own towels as the ones the hospital has aren't the best. Maybe a robe, slippers, comfy socks." Heidi rattles off and I move that mental list to a list on my phone, so I don't forget anything.

"Got it all written down," I say. "Anything else you can think of?"

"Chargers, a tablet or laptop for movies, or just surfing the internet. Kindle or some books to read, deck of cards for playing with visitors or when alone. You're allowed to order food if you don't want to eat the hospital food all the time. Oh, don't let me forget to bring you the menu. You can pick and choose what you want rather than getting whatever the default meal for the day is. As long as you submit your requests by the deadline on each one, you can pick and choose," Heidi tells us.

"Sounds great. Are they strict about the visitors' hours for this floor?" Raven asks.

"We try to be a little more relaxed as long as you aren't in any distress. The immediate family can be here at any time, so Dad can be here whenever he wants. We can even wheel in a chair that folds down into a bed if you want to stay overnight at some point."

"Do you want me to run home now to pack you a bag and bring you some things to have?" I ask Raven. I know she's in good hands here in the hospital.

"Yeah, the sooner, the better I suppose." She smiles at me. "I think I have a load of laundry in the dryer, so can you check there for my favorite lounge pants that still fit."

"How about I just FaceTime you when I get home, and you can tell me exactly what to pack."

"You've got yourself a good one," Heidi says. "He's resourceful."

"I just don't want to bring the wrong things," I chuckle. "I know how pregnancy hormones work," I tease.

"Now, now. No harping on the pregnancy hormones," Heidi teases back.

"Do you want me to bring you some lunch when I come back?" I ask Raven.

"Yes, please. I'll decide by the time you FaceTime me what I want."

"Sounds like a plan. I'll call Camden and fill him in on what's going on," I tell her.

"Okay, see you soon. Love you," Raven says before I kiss her goodbye and head out the door.

"Why'd you skip out on practice?" Camden says as soon as he accepts my call. "All Coach said was you took a personal day."

"Raven had an appointment and is back in the hospital until she has the baby," I say and am met with silence. My eyes flick to the screen on my dash to make sure the call wasn't dropped. "You still there, man?" I ask.

"Yeah, how's she doing?" he asks.

"Her spirits were upbeat for the most part. She kind of fell apart for a few minutes but was doing good when I just left a few minutes ago. I'm running home to pack her a bag. We didn't have anything with us since all we'd left for was her normal doctor's appointment."

"I can head over to keep her company. I'm just leaving the rink now," he offers.

"I'm sure she'd like that. I'll hopefully be back in an hour or so. Told her I'd FaceTime so she can pick what I bring her."

"Smart thinking," he chuckles.

"I was also going to text the girls' group and see if they can set up a schedule to visit her. Especially when we have to leave in a few days. Fuck, man, I don't know if I tell Coach I need a few personal days and stay behind, but I also don't want to put the team in a bind."

"Go talk to him. I'm sure the two of you can come up with a plan. Family comes first."

"I'll give him a call once I get things to the hospital and Raven settled in for the night."

"Don't forget to take care of yourself in the meantime. You are no good to her if you aren't on your game."

"I'll try to remember that," I tell him as I pull into my neighborhood.

"I'll see you when you get back to the hospital. I'm headed there now," Camden says before we end our call.

Once home, I pull out a duffel bag and put it on the bed. I also find a backpack and place Raven's Kindle in there along with her iPad. I find the chargers for both and add them to the bag. I go in search of her laptop and put that in as well. I check the list I made and start grabbing the things Heidi suggested like a few towels, Raven's toiletries, some slippers, and her robe and place them all on the bed. I grab the clothes from the dryer and fold them quickly so I can easily show them to her when I call in just a few minutes. I pull out some of her other clothes from the dresser and closet and add them to the bed so she can pick and choose.

I grab my phone and tap her contact. The phone rings twice before her beautiful face fills the screen. "Ready to tell me what to pack?" I ask.

"Sure am," she says.

"I already put your electronics and all their chargers in the backpack. On the bed, I have all the clothes from the dryer plus some from your closet on the bed to hopefully make it easier for you to see and pick from," I explain before I turn the camera around. We start with one side of the bed, and I make my way through everything I have laid out, moving things into a pack pile and no piles.

"I think I have a newer pair of slippers in the closet. Can you check for those?" she asks.

"Yep," I say as I walk into the closet and scan her side looking for them.

"Down there on the bottom, in that plastic bag," she says, and I see the package she's talking about. I grab it and sure enough, it is a new pair of slippers.

"Anything else you can think of for this trip?"

"Did you grab my lotion off the nightstand?"

"Not yet, but I can," I say, walking back out and adding it to the growing pile of things to bring. At this point, I'm going to need a full suitcase, not just a duffel bag. "Do you want me to bring the baby bag yet?"

"No, you can grab it later, or just put it in the car maybe?" she suggests.

"That's a good idea," I say, making a mental note to do just that.

"Do you want your pregnancy pillow?"

"Absolutely."

"Can you think of anything else?"

"Not at the moment."

"Okay, I'm going to see how best to get all this stuff packed up. I'll call you before I leave to make sure you haven't thought of anything else you'd like me to bring this time."

"Thanks, babe," she says before we disconnect.

I take the duffel bag back to the closet and swap it for a suitcase. Thankfully, I'm able to fit everything in there and the backpack I already put things into. I check the bathroom again, making sure I've grabbed most of her necessary toiletries.

"Done already?" she asks upon answering my call.

"Almost, just doing one last check for anything obvious. I grabbed toiletries and your shower stuff, but did you want your makeup bag?"

"No, but can you make sure I've got some hair ties and at least one of my clips to put my hair up with?"

"Already packed those," I tell her.

"Then I think I'm all set."

"Have you decided on lunch?" I ask.

"Can you grab some tacos from somewhere on your way here? Maybe a side of chips and salsa as well."

"Sure can. Do you want anything to drink?"

"My usual from Starbies, please."

I chuckle. "I didn't even need to ask I suppose."

"I'm going to miss being able to go whenever I feel like it."

"There's always delivery," I remind her.

"Maybe when I'm desperate."

"I'm sure one of the girls would be happy to swing by Starbucks daily for you and bring it by," I suggest.

"That's a good idea. I'll text the group chat to see who's up for it."

"Have you told them already that you're back in the hospital?" I ask.

"Not yet, but I'm going to as soon as I get off the phone with you. Camden is here with me now."

"Does he want some lunch?" I ask and I hear her ask him in return.

"He says he'll text you what he wants."

"Sounds good. I'll see you soon."

I slip my phone into my pocket and sling the backpack strap over my shoulder, then grab the top handle of the suitcase and make my way downstairs. I grab one of Raven's favorite cups with a straw just in case she'd rather use that than the hospital's Styrofoam ones.

I look up a Mexican restaurant between the house and the hospital and after looking at their menu, I quickly send a link to Camden so he can tell me what he wants. I also verify that Raven wants the beef tacos today, as the last thing I want to do is order the wrong kind.

> Can you come down to the parking lot and help me get all this stuff up to the room when I get there?

I shoot off the text to Camden before I leave the restaurant and drive the few miles to the hospital. He's waiting outside the main doors when I drive past, so I pull over into the drop off area and hand off the to-go bags of food and drinks. "I can get the rest," I tell him before I go in search of a parking spot.

CHAPTER 22
RAVEN

Hey ladies. Don't freak out, but I wanted to let all of you know I'm back in the hospital. This time until I deliver, we're hoping that it is in a few weeks, but it might be much sooner.

AVERY

Oh honey, I'm so sorry. Please let us know what we can do to help! We're here for you for anything, especially when the guys are on the road.

TORI

So sorry to hear that. How are you feeling? Just say the word and we're there. How about a watch party on Friday night in your room?

I'm feeling okay, just tired and frustrated my blood pressure won't stay down. I'm in a permanent room and Blake ran home to pack me some stuff. A watch party sounds great, but we have to keep it calm for my health.

KENDRA

Oh man, I'm so sorry. I'm happy to help however I can. Do you want some meals delivered to you? Is that allowed?

That's so thoughtful of you. I don't know if I have access to heat anything up, but my nurse did say I can order in delivery if I want something other than hospital food.

KENDRA

I can easily pack you up at least a meal a day and bring it to you.

AVERY

Maybe we can set up a rotation based on who's available when. Make sure you get at least one visitor a day. Someone who can bring you a treat and some girl time.

I don't know what I did to deserve all of you, but I'm truly thankful.

I switch out of the group chat and send one to Tess, knowing I needed to update her as well.

Back in the hospital, this time until I deliver this baby.

> Well, fuck a duck. I'm so sorry. Want me to fly up and come hang out for few days?

> I mean I won't tell you no, but I also don't want you to drop everything to be here if it is inconvenient.

> Say no more. I'll have a flight booked within the hour. You're never an inconvenience to me.

> Blake will be gone for a few days later this week, so if you want to wait a few days to come, it would be nice to have you here then.

> Of course, I'll check his schedule and plan a trip. Keep me posted on how you're doing in the meantime.

> Will do. Love and miss you.

> Love and miss you as well. Tell that niece of mine that she needs to hold tight for a few more weeks.

> Doing my best!

AND NOW TO LET MY PARENTS KNOW WHAT'S GOING ON. I click on the family group chat.

> Back in the hospital for the foreseeable future, well at least until this little one makes her debut.

MOM

Oh sweetie, I'm sorry. Do you want dad and I to fly out early?

DAD

Just say the word and I'll change our tickets.

I think you can wait a little longer. Change your flights if I end up going into labor early. I really want you guys here once she is born. Not much anyone can do for me while I'm chained to the hospital bed.

CAMDEN

I'll keep an eye on her for you guys. Currently sitting in her room as we type this. Kind of weird to be texting with someone I'm right next to. {laughing emoji}

Smart ass.

MOM

Thank you for being there for her. I knew I raised you both right.

DAD

You weren't saying that when they were teenagers and fighting all the time.

I can't help but laugh out loud at our parents' banter back and forth.

"They'll never let us live those years down, will they?" Camden asks.

"Nope, and I'm sure they'll tell our kids all about how we were growing up."

The door opens and Blake walks in, a full-size suitcase behind him and a backpack slung over his shoulder. "I have the goods," he jokes as he rolls over to the little closet area my room has. "Do you want me to put things away for you?" he asks.

"That'd be great, but come eat first," I tell him. The food smells amazing and my stomach is growling. Camden opens the bags and starts distributing the food between the three of us. Thankfully this room is on the larger side and has a two-seat couch, a small table with two chairs, along with the closet area with a small center for us to store things. My private bathroom also has some extra storage areas, which come in handy when you're admitted to the hospital for weeks at a time.

"Tess is going to come up for a few days. Probably this weekend when you guys are on the road," I tell the guys.

"That's a good plan. I'm still worried about leaving you. I was considering talking to Coach about taking some personal days, so I didn't have to leave town."

"While I love the thought, you need to be with your team. I'm in the best hands here. I have a slew of amazing women who are already planning on who's visiting me on what day so that I always have someone checking in on me. They also want to come here for our watch party this weekend."

"That is comforting, but I still don't want to miss the birth."

"And I don't want you to either, but I have a good

feeling that she's going to stay put for at least a few more weeks." I tell him as I rub my belly. "There is something the two of you can do for me." I say, looking between Blake and Camden.

"Anything, darlin'," Blake says.

"Finish setting up the nursery. I'd like to come home to it finished if possible."

"Consider it done," Camden says.

I LIE IN MY HOSPITAL BED, THE DAYS ALL RUNNING together at this point. But I'm thankful for my Shockwaves family. The other wives and girlfriends have been my lifesavers since being admitted. Last night after the guys left town, Avery, Tori, and Kendra all came over and hung out for a while. They brought me dinner and a lovely gift basket filled with so many amazing things from snacks to skin care products. A new set of the most conformable lounge pants and top. Seriously, these women are amazing.

"Knock, knock," a voice I'd know from anywhere calls out as my door opens. "Honey, I'm home," Tess says as she walks fully into my room. It is so good to see her again. I haven't seen her since I surprised her at her birthday party.

"You made it!" I wiggle in the bed, excited to see my best friend. It was strange not being able to go pick her up at the airport, but based on the suitcase behind her, she came here straight from the airport.

"Of course, I did! I was up and ready to go to the airport hours early. Jeremy was laughing at me." She says as she comes over and wraps me in a huge hug. "Look at how good you look! I wish I looked this good when spending all day in bed." She rests a hand on my stomach as she sits on the edge of my bed.

"Not how I thought my pregnancy would go, but I'm thankful for every day that she stays inside. I just really hope she comes when Blake is home. He really struggled with if he should go with the team or not. He met with his coach, the general manager, and the team owner to discuss his options. The owner made him a deal that if I was to go into labor, they'd put him on his private jet and get him back home ASAP. So to accommodate that, Nathan is flying on his jet rather than just going with the team so that the plane is always with them."

"That's some commitment to him and shows just how much they value him."

"It really does and made him a little less nervous. I also promised I'd alert them of any changes. Trinity, the team's social media manager is my first point of contact if they are in practice or at the game. She's even been texting me to check in randomly since they left."

"Aww, how sweet. I'm so glad you found such an amazing second family here. Have you made any decisions around returning to work after Abby is born?" Tess asks. She's one of the only people I've talked to about Blake and me having the conversation of me staying home with her.

"I haven't talked to my bosses yet, but it is really tempting. While being on bed rest is going to be completely different than being home with a newborn, I just can't wrap my mind around leaving her every day, but I also busted my ass to graduate and make a name for myself at my firm. It feels kind of strange to just give all of that up."

"That is understandable, but you can always go back after a few years if you wanted to. Maybe stay home until Blake retires and then go back part time?" she suggests.

"That's an idea to consider. I'm not ready to make any rash decisions."

"Nor should you. So what do you want for lunch? I'm starving, so let's order something."

"Sushi?" I suggest, knowing she never turns it down.

"Um, yes. But can you eat it?" She asks.

"As long as I get cooked things, I can. Just nothing raw."

"Perfect, do you have a place in mind?" she asks.

"Of course, and they deliver, so even better." I pull out my phone and pull them up on the delivery app. We place our order and visit until our food is delivered.

I SIT NERVOUSLY ON THE BED AS WE WATCH THE TIME TICK down on the play clock. The Shockwaves are in Philadelphia and currently up 1-0 with only a minute left in the game. Philly has pulled their goalie to put an extra attacker out on the ice.

The ref blows the whistle, the Philly line was offsides as they attempted to gain the zone. While the guys all line up on the ice for the face off, I look around at all the women filling my room. They brought our normal watch party to me and have done a great job keeping things light and fun, so my blood pressure doesn't go haywire.

"Come on, guys," I hear Tori mumble under her breath.

We all watch with rapt attention as the puck is dropped again, and this time Philly gains the zone. Everyone spreads out, and they pass the puck between players as they attempt to find an opening. A few attempts go wide, and another right into Blake's chest. He holds the puck, so the whistle blows again, this time with only twelve seconds left on the clock.

They drop the puck and Ryker is able to push it wide and back into the corner. Three players all converge on it, tying it up against the boards as the final seconds tick off the clock. As soon as the buzzer goes off, signaling the game is over, Blake's arms shoot straight up into the air, another win under his belt. I'm so glad he went. He needed this so much more than he realized.

"Woohoo!" Someone calls out in the room, celebrating the guys win tonight. Everyone is high fiving one another, and they all make sure to include me as they move about the room.

"It was so nice to meet you," Avery says to Tess. "I'm glad you were able to make it into town this weekend. We've been doing our best to keep Raven company since she was admitted, but I know having another friendly face is helpful."

"No where else I'd rather be," she replies as she leans into my side. I have an extra-large hospital bed, and when I move to one side, I can fit someone next to me if they don't mind being close enough our sides touch.

"Did you want one of us to stop by tomorrow?" Kendra asks.

"Y'all can take the weekend off if you want. I'll be here except when I'm sleeping," Tess offers.

"Sounds good. Just call or text if you need anything. Food or company, it doesn't matter," Kendra offers.

"Thank you all so much for everything," I say, getting a little misty eyed. I'd go crazy if it wasn't for everyone in this room keeping me sane lately.

The girls all clean up the food trays they brought and leave shortly after. It's back to just Tess and me, until she decided to head back to the house and get some sleep, promising to return in the morning with some breakfast.

CHAPTER 23
BLAKE
THREE WEEKS LATER

"Blake," Trinity, our social media manager calls my name as I come off the ice from practice today. She's got a mischievous grin on her face which makes me a little nervous.

"Yes," I say, stopping in front of her where she's holding up the tiny microphone she likes using when making the behind-the-scenes videos she uses a for the team's social media accounts.

"Got a quick question for you today," she says.

"Don't you always," I tease. I'm at ease as the last few weeks have been kind of strange. Raven has done amazing since being admitted to the hospital. The bed rest and constant monitoring have worked how we hoped they would and kept the baby in. She's only a week from her due date, so anytime now, it could be go time.

"What's your thoughts on becoming a dad today?"

She asks and it takes a few seconds for her question to really sink in.

"She's in labor?" I ask. I can feel the smile reach my eyes. I'll be meeting my baby girl today.

"She is, called about thirty minutes ago. Said it's early, so you have plenty of time to shower and get over to the hospital." Trinity tells me as I take off for the locker room.

I strip from my gear and make it into the shower in record time. "Where's the fire?" One of the guys calls after me.

"Raven's in labor. I got to go!" I call out to everyone in the locker room.

"She is, since when?" Camden asks from outside the shower bays.

"Trinity said she got the call about a half hour ago, so not long," I tell him all I know.

"Sweet, keep me posted. I'll wait at home for your call or text," he says once I'm out of the shower and pulling clean clothes on.

"Will do," I tell him as I clap him on the back.

"Blake," Coach calls out as he enters the locker room. "I see you've heard the news. Congratulations. Keep me posted and we'll make the call tomorrow morning if we need to bring up a backup for the game so you can have the night away from the rink. I'll let you make that call, but if it's any help, I planned to start Stubbs tomorrow night, so you'd be on the bench."

"Thanks, Coach. I'll keep that in mind and let you

know," I tell him before I grab my bag and go tearing out of the practice facility and straight to my car.

I make it to the hospital and directly up to Raven's room. They've got her hooked up to a new monitor that appears to be recording her contractions.

"Hey, darlin'," I greet as I lean down and kiss her, all while pressing a hand to her belly. "How are you feeling?"

"So ready to hold this little one on the outside," she says, looking so happy and content even though she's in labor.

"You're doing so good, such a badass," I tell her as a contraction peaks on the monitor screen.

The next few hours fly by. Raven's contractions come faster and get stronger. Dr. Davis finally makes an appearance after the nurse's last check, showing that she was almost ready to start pushing.

"Let's get this baby out," Dr. Davis says as he takes a seat on the doctor's stool at the end of the bed. At some point the nurses did something to remove a portion of the bed and expose the stirrups.

I hold back one of Raven's legs while one of the nurses helps hold the other. "On the count of three, I want you to give me a big push," Dr. Davis instructs.

"One, two, three," one of the nurses calls out and Raven pulls in a big breath and curls forward, pushing with all her might.

"That's great!" the nurse encourages her. "A few more like that and you'll be all done," she tells her.

"And again," the doctor calls out, and we repeat.

"On the next contraction, I want you to give half the push to get the head out, then we can push again after I make sure the cord isn't wrapped," he says and Raven nods her understanding.

"You're doing so good," I praise her. "I love you, darlin'." I kiss her temple just as she curls forward again, pushing just as the doctor instructed. I look down and see our daughter's head appear. The doctor quickly sweeps his fingers around the neck and slips the umbilical cord over my daughter's neck.

"Okay, final push," Dr. Davis says, and Raven gives it all she's got. The next few seconds are a blur as they set Abby on Raven's chest. Her little cries fill the room and tears fill my eyes.

"You did it, babe." I kiss Raven's temple again.

"She's so cute," Raven says as she looks at our daughter on her chest. Her little cries stop as she hears Raven's voice. Her little eyes look up and I swear my heart beats out of my chest at that moment. Seeing my daughter and the love my life in this precious moment together.

"Would you like to cut the cord, Blake?" Dr. Davis asks.

"Absolutely," I say, moving my attention to the special scissors one of the nurses is holding for me to take.

The next few hours are also a whirlwind as friends and family start to arrive to come meet our new bundle of joy. Both Raven's and my parents flew in, both choosing to come in a few days ago so they wouldn't miss out on seeing their grand baby as soon as she was born. Thankfully they have been staying at the house and our mothers both put the final touches on the nursery just today.

I sit on the side of the bed, holding my daughter on my chest as she snoozes away. Raven nursed her, then handed her over for a diaper change and to be burped. I gladly took her, holding her like the precious bundle that she is.

"You look good with a baby on your chest," Raven says, pulling my attention to her.

"Yeah?" I ask.

"Best view I've seen in a long time," she smiles sweetly at me. The exhaustion of the day, hell, the last month is noticeable. She's such a badass with everything she's dealt with, all with a smile on her face and a determination to get our baby here safely.

"I love you." I say, other words failing me now as I think over everything she's been through.

"I love you, too. Thanks for keeping me sane these last few weeks. I could've have done all this without you."

"You're the one that deserves all the praise. You're amazing."

"I'm so ready to go home," she says.

"I bet you are. Hopefully tomorrow," I tell her.

"It can't come soon enough. I miss our bed. It will be strange to not be tied to a hospital bed all day and night."

"I can only imagine."

"And our shower. I've had dreams of returning to our shower," she muses, a dreamy look on her face.

"What about snuggling up to me at night?" I ask, feeling a little left out.

"Well, I guess," she teases.

"I see how it is. You just said yes to me because of my shower head."

"It is pretty magical." She keeps the teasing going.

"I'll show you magical, darlin'." I wiggle my eyebrows at her.

"I'd throw something at you if you weren't holding Abby right now," she laughs. "No touchy touchy for at least six, maybe eight weeks. I have to heal first and I'm not ready to get knocked up by you again." She says sternly.

"I know, I know. And this one is enough for us for now," I agree. Her body has been through enough. I fully agree that another baby isn't something we need for a while.

SHOCKWAVES

"WHAT DO YOU SAY WE BUST YOU OUT OF THIS PLACE?" Heidi says when she comes into the room the next morning.

"I say yes!" Raven cheers quietly as Abby is sleeping on her lap.

"Dr. Davis would like to see you in one week, and Miss Abby here should be seen by her pediatrician within a week as well. Just give both offices a call and make those appointments at your convenience," Heidi explains. "I'll get your IV port removed and then you can start getting ready to head home. Just let me know when you are, and I'll call for the wheelchair.

"Thank you so much for everything," Raven says once Heidi removes her IV port. They unhooked the IVs yesterday, just left the port just in case they needed to give her anything else before discharge. Thankfully her body is bouncing back after delivery and showing no signs of the pre-eclampsia since then.

"It was truly my pleasure, along with all the other nurses. We enjoyed having you here. And you got yourself such a cutie," Heidi says, as she looks down at Abby who's sleeping peacefully.

"Thanks. We happen to agree," Raven says about our daughter.

I get to work packing up everything that we need to take home. I swear every time someone stopped by, they brought new things with them. It takes me multiple loads to get everything down to the SUV. On my last trip back up to the room, I brought Abby's car seat with me so we could get her secured into it. I stopped at a local fire station last week to have them verify it was installed properly, which it was.

"All right, let's get out before they change their minds," I joke with Raven.

"I never thought this moment would arrive," Raven says as she takes a seat in the wheelchair. I carry the car seat while Raven is pushed by the wheelchair attendant to the front doors where they wait for me to pull the SUV around to the loading area.

"Are you sitting up front with me or in the back with Abby?" I ask after clicking the car seat into the base.

"Like that's even a question you have to ask? In the back with Abby." She smiles at me.

I help her up into the seat, then wait for her seatbelt to be secure before I shut the door. I jump into the driver's seat and drive the slowest I've ever driven as I take the two most precious people home, where our parents and Camden are all waiting for us to arrive.

CHAPTER 24
RAVEN
TWO MONTHS LATER

I stand up as I sway back and forth with Abby. She's such an amazing baby, which I've been thankful for after such a challenging last half of my pregnancy. The Shockwaves shocked everyone by making it all the way to the finals, and they are currently less than two minutes away from winning it all.

"I don't know if I will survive another two minutes," Avery says beside me. All the families are watching the game from a suite for today's game. Most of the older kids are running around playing amongst each other as all their moms watch their loved one down on the ice fighting for the ultimate prize in hockey.

"Same. I keep debating turning away, but I just can't peel my eyes off the ice."

"They've got this," Tori chimes in. "They are so laser focused."

"I know. I have faith," I say. They are currently up

by two goals and dominating the puck over Buffalo. Both teams that made it to the finals were surprises in their own right. Buffalo coming into the playoffs as the wild card for their division and the Shockwaves as the newest team in the league. Every critic said a new team wouldn't ever be good enough in their first ten seasons, at minimum, to make it to the playoffs, better yet win a cup. This is only their fourth season, and we're down to a minute between them and a cup win to prove all those critics wrong.

"Ten, nine, eight," one of the kids starts counting down as the time on the clock ticks down. The suite goes wild as do the guys on the ice as the final buzzer goes off. I keep my eyes on Blake as his glove, blocker, helmet and stick all go flying into the air, just as everyone else's stuff does. His entire team surrounds him in the largest pile as they all celebrate their amazing win.

We all watch with tears in our eyes as they present the team with the Cup. Ryker skates over and after a picture with the cup and the league commissioner, he's handed the cup to take his celebratory lap around the rink. The home crowd goes wild as Ryker skates around. He hands it off to Aiden next, who takes his lap and continues passing it along. I take out my phone and record as first Blake, then Camden, take their lap around the rink.

"Everyone that would like to go congratulate the guys on the ice are welcome to head down at this time," one of the front office staff members calls out.

I have Abby in a baby carrier that is strapped to my chest, so I grab my pass and head for the elevator. Security escorts us from the elevator to the rink, allowing the family members to walk out on the ice that is covered with carpet now so we don't slip on the ice. I look through the crowd of people on the ice for either Blake or my brother. Blake sees me and comes skating over, before I know what he's doing, he's wrapped his arms around me and lifts me up, skating both Abby and me in circles. "You did it!" I place both my hands on his sweaty cheeks. "You fucking did it!"

"We did, darlin', I still can't believe it."

"You deserve it. You played so good!" I tell him before leaning in for a kiss. It isn't the easiest kiss since he's still in his huge pads and we have a baby between us, but our lips connect for a few seconds.

Blake sets me back down and makes sure I've got my footing beneath me before he lets go. He unclips the carrier and takes Abby out so he can hold her. It melts my heart to see the two of them together. He's such a great dad, always tending to her when he's home. Getting up with us in the middle of the night when she wakes up to eat.

"Hey, sis," Camden comes skating over and wraps me in a hug.

"Congratulations. I'm so proud of you!" I tell him.

"Thanks. It's surreal, that's for sure!"

Our parents join us in the celebration, and eventually we have a moment as a family to take a picture of

Blake, Abby, and me with the cup. It seems to be tradition that players put their babies in the cup for pictures.

The party goes on for hours, and I finally head home, leaving the guys to celebrate late into the night with their teammates.

Blake

THE LAST WEEK HAS BEEN A WHIRLWIND. WE PARTIED ALL night long after winning the cup, and those parties never seemed to stop for the following four days, leading up to the day of the parade. The city went wild and came out in droves to celebrate with all of us. Riding on the floats, seeing all the fans, and then ending the parade outside the arena where we continued partying for a few more hours. I'll never forget those days or what it felt like to be a cup champion.

Now that the parties have stopped and some of the guys have all started to head home for the short off season, I've taken advantage of these last few days to just soak up time with my family. Both my parents and Raven's came out for the finals, but they're all going home tomorrow. So tonight, they are watching Abby so the two of us can go out on a kid free date. It's been forever since we got to go out, just the two of us, so I'm looking forward to some time alone.

"Hot momma!" I whistle as Raven comes out of the

bathroom. She's got on a summer dress that shows off her curves. I've always thought she was beautiful, no matter what, and by the way my cock is already hard, that hasn't changed one bit since she gave birth.

"Oh, hush," she winks at me as she slips an earring into her lobe. "Where are you taking me tonight?" she asks.

"Out," I say, as I haven't told her where yet. I was able to score some reservations at one of the nicest steak houses in San Francisco that usually has a few months wait. When they heard my name, it was amazing how quickly they found me an open table. I don't usually try to use my clout for things like this, but tonight is different.

"You don't say." She deadpans, giving me a look.

"It's a surprise, just like the rest of the night is." I wrap my arm around her and pull her close. My cock presses against her belly and the gasp tells me she feels it.

"I'm ready," she says and I don't think she's meaning to leave for dinner. She was finally cleared by her doctor a week ago for sex, but with my schedule and her hesitancy, we haven't tried anything yet. To say I'm ready is an understatement, but I'd wait for her forever if that's what it took.

"Me too, darlin'. Later tonight, I'll make you feel so damn good," I promise.

"Can we skip right to that part?" she asks, and I almost consider ditching our dinner plans and going straight to the hotel I have booked.

"No can do. I need you well fed to have the stamina you'll need to make it through the night."

"Then let's go," she says and pulls from my arms.

I grab the overnight bag, along with her pump bag and follow her out of the room. When we get downstairs, I find our mothers sitting next to one another on the couch, Abby lying on my mom's legs as both women coo at her. Now that she's a few months old, she's starting to stay awake for longer stretches of time and is starting to interact with us a little more.

"It's time to say goodbye to Mommy and Daddy," my mom tells Abby. I take her from my mom's lap and snuggle her close.

"Daddy loves you, baby girl. You be good tonight for Grammy, Grandma, Pops, and Grandpa. I want good reports," I tell my daughter.

"Hand her over," Raven tells me. She's always calling me a baby hog, but who can blame a guy when he's got such a cute kid?

I do as I'm asked. "Love you, love bug," Raven says before kissing Abby and handing her back over to the waiting grandparents.

"You two have a good night out; we've got everything under control here at home."

"Thank you all so much," Raven says to our parents.

I'm not sure which one of us is more nervous about leaving Abby for the night, and it isn't because we don't trust our parents, but because this will be the first time we're both away from her overnight.

I slide my hand over and rest it on Raven's thigh.

Her dress is long enough that I can't slip underneath it, not that that would be a good idea while I'm driving us to dinner.

"She'll be fine, babe," I say to break the silence.

Raven blows out a breath. "I know, but it still doesn't change the fact my mind is racing about leaving her all night."

"Just give me a couple of hours and I'll have your mind off Abby and on other things."

Raven squirms under my palm and I know she's just as ready as I am to be intimate again.

"Did you seriously get reservations at House of Prime?" Raven asks when we pull up to the valet station.

"I did." I confirm as both our doors are opened. I hand the valet some cash as he hands me the claim ticket and we're shown inside the upscale restaurant.

"Mr. Watson, thank you for dining with us this evening. We have your table ready for you," the manager says as he escorts the two of us directly back to a secluded table.

"Thank you very much," I say as he hands us the menus.

"Good evening. I'm Edward, and I'll be your head server tonight. Can I start you out with a cocktail or something from the bar?"

"Darlin', would you like something from the bar?" I ask Raven.

"I'll take the lemon drop," she says after looking over the drink menu.

"Perfect choice, ma'am. And for you, sir?" Edward asks.

"I'll have an amber beer, whatever you have on tap."

"Of course. I'll be back shortly with your drinks."

"Have you ever been here?" Raven asks.

"Once, my first season here. Nathan booked the entire restaurant and brought everyone here for a meal."

"Wow! Someone was talking about it at work not long after I started, so I looked it up, but that's all I'd heard about this place."

"After tonight, you can say you've experienced it," I tell her. My nerves are starting to build with the little box that is in my pocket. Tonight is going to be special in more ways than one. I just have to wait for the right moment to drop to one knee and ask the biggest question of my life.

DINNER IS SPECTACULAR, JUST LIKE I REMEMBERED IT BEING when I was here a few years ago.

"Are you ready?" I ask Raven. I've paid the bill and we've both eaten more than enough.

"I was born ready." She smirks at me from across the table.

"Then what are we waiting for?" I quirk a brow.

I stand and help pull her chair out so she can also stand. She slips her hand into mine and I lead her out of the restaurant. My car is already waiting for us when we reach the front door, so I just hand over a tip with the claim ticket as Raven slips into the passenger seat. I slide into the driver's seat and we're back on the road within a few minutes. I punch in the hotel on my GPS, and it doesn't take us long to pull in there. Like at the restaurant, I hand over my keys with a tip to the valet, and he hands me a claim ticket. Before we head into the hotel, I grab the two bags from the back seat, and we head inside to check in for the night.

"Welcome to the Ritz Carlton. Thank you for staying with us tonight, Mr. Watson. We have you in the penthouse suite. Everything you requested is already in the room. Should you need anything additional sent up, please don't hesitate to call our concierge desk. They are here for you at any hour, day or night."

"Thank you," I say as I take our keys.

I swear the tension between Raven and me rises as the elevator up to the penthouse rises. "I can't wait to see that dress on the floor," I growl as I pull her closer to me. My lips find her exposed neck and press kisses to her skin. I've wanted to do this all night but have behaved myself until now.

"I'd like to see this on the floor myself," she says, tugging at my button-up shirt.

The elevator dings when we arrive on the top floor. The door swooshes open and our door is only a few feet away. I swipe the key across the electronic pad and our doors open.

"Oh my," Raven says, shock filling her voice as she steps into the suite, her hand covering her mouth as she takes a few more steps forward and sees all the flowers I had delivered and set up in the living room. They lead over next to the floor to ceiling window that has the perfect view of the city skyline. Hanging down in front of the windows is a neon sign that lights up as Raven walks toward it that reads, *Will you marry me?*

When the sign blinks to life, she stops dead in her tracks, and she turns to find me down on one knee behind her.

"Darlin', we might have met in the most cliché way, but that night turned our lives upside down, and I'd like to think for the better. You gave me—us—a chance to see where this would go, gave us a chance to become a family. You gave me the most precious thing ever— our daughter, and for that I'll forever be grateful. I love you with all my heart, Raven Rowe. Now I'm asking you to do forever with me as my wife. Will you marry me, darlin'?"

"Yes!" Raven cries as she bends down to cup my cheeks and press her lips to mine. I wrap an arm around her torso and stand up, taking her with me as I do. We kiss for a long time before breaking apart. "I didn't even look at the ring," she laughs. "I would have said yet with a paper ring if it meant spending the rest of my life with you," she tells me. I set her back down so I can take the ring out of the box and slip it on her finger.

"I love you," I tell her again as I slip the ring on.

"Not as much as I love you," she tells me. "It's gorgeous, Blake. Absolutely gorgeous."

"Before I take you into the bedroom and have my wicked way with you, do you need to pump first?" I ask.

"As unsexy as that is, yes. I'm feeling extremely full right now."

"There's a mini fridge over by the wet bar that I had them bring in just for you to store the milk ."

"You really did think of everything, didn't you?"

"I wanted this night to be perfect," I shrug my shoulders as I hand over her pump bag. She gets situated on the couch and hooks up the pump. Thankfully it doesn't take her super long and before I know it, she's cleaning up and putting everything away for now.

"Excuses me, Fiancé," Raven says as she saunters back over to where I'm waiting on the couch.

"Yes, darlin'?"

"I'm ready for you to take me to bed." She bats her eyelashes at me, and my cock stirs behind my zipper.

"Are you sure?" I purr.

"I've never been surer about anything in my life."

I don't hesitate a second longer. I stand up and swoop her into my arms and head straight for the bed.

"Strip, now," I command once we're standing at the end of the bed. I don't have the patience to peel off our clothes slowly tonight. Raven must not either as she starts removing her clothes just as fast as I do.

"You're already so hard," she says as her palm wraps around my shaft.

"Fuck," I hiss, the contact already putting me on

edge. It's been so long since I've been inside her. Once she was put on bed rest, we couldn't do anything.

"Yes, I'd like you to fuck me," Raven says, pulling me closer.

"Such a dirty mouth you have tonight," I say before kissing her. My tongue instantly finds hers as we kiss and touch like we're long-lost lovers. I pick her up slightly and set her on the edge of the bed, our lips never losing contact as our kiss deepens.

Her hand stokes me slowly. Every time her palm slides across my tip, I can feel as another bead of pre-cum wets my crown. "Fuck, baby," I say into her flesh. "That feels so fucking good." I kiss a path down her body, stopping only momentarily to nip at her nipples. I don't need a face full of milk, so I leave them alone as I travel further down her body. "Open wider for me, darlin'," I tell her as I tap on her inner thighs. She complies and I drop to my knees. I press kisses to her inner thighs, and they start to quiver.

"I'm already almost going to come," Raven says as she pushes up on her elbows to look down at me between her thighs.

"Not yet, I need to taste you first," I say as my tongue darts out and slides up her folds. "Hmm," I groan at her sweetness.

"Blake," she cries out my name as I lap at her center again. This time I find her clit and suck it lightly. "Yes," she cries as I push a finger inside. Between finding her g-spot from the inside and my mouth on her clit, she detonates instantly. Her legs wrap tightly around my head, and I keep sucking and rubbing until she jerks away.

"Feel good?" I ask as I press kisses to her inner thighs again.

"So good," she says blissfully.

I walk over to the overnight bag and grab the box of condoms I remembered to toss in. I open it up, pulling out a packet, which I tear open and roll down my cock. Once I'm sheathed, I return to the bed and crawl on beside Raven. "Are you ready for more?"

"Are you going to fuck me now?" she asks, still a little lost in her orgasmic haze.

"No, I'm going to make love to you for the first time as my fiancée," I correct.

"Yes, please," she says as I roll over her body and hover above.

"Look at me, darlin'," I say and her eyes pop open and connect with mine. "I promise to always make you a priority, to always be by your side, to support you and our family. To support your dreams and aspirations, no matter how big or small they are." I pour my heart out to this woman who has done so much for me in the last year.

It's funny how fate works sometimes. Seeing as it was this exact date, just one year ago that we were in a hotel room in Vegas doing just this that led to everything else.

I push inside my future bride. "God damn, you're going to make me come," I grit out as I start pumping in and out.

"Hopefully." She half laughs, half moans as I hike her leg up higher on my hip and hit just a little deeper. My thumb finds her clit and I rub circles around it as my pace increases.

"I'm going to come," I warn her. "You'd better come on this cock before I fill you up."

"Blake," she cries out and pulls me right over the edge with her.

I flop to the mattress, my body spent.

"Ready for forever, future Mrs. Watson?"

"I'm ready," she agrees.

ARE YOU READY TO HIT THE GRIDIRON? UP NEXT FROM Samantha Lind is a brand new series featuring some sexy football players who will be heating up the field in 2024! Pre-order the first book in the series today!

COMING SOON

To find out what's next from Samantha, please visit her website at samanthalind.com

ALSO BY SAMANTHA LIND

INDIANAPOLIS EAGLES SERIES

Just Say Yes ~ Scoring The Player

Playing For Keeps ~ Protecting Her Heart

Against The Boards ~ The First Intermission

The Hardest Shot ~ The Game Changer

Rookie Move ~ The Final Period

Box Set 1 {Books 1-3} ~ Box Set 2 {Books 4-6}

Box Set 3 {Books 7-10}

INDIANAPOLIS LIGHTNING SERIES

The Perfect Pitch ~ The Curve Ball

The Screw Ball ~ The Change Up

LYRICS & LOVE SERIES

Marry Me ~ Drunk Girl

Rumor Going 'Round ~ Just A Kiss

STANDALONE TITLES

Tempting Tessa

Then You Came Along

When I Found You

Cocky Doc

SWEET VALLEY, TENNESSEE

Nothing Bundt Love

Nothing Bundt Forever

SAN FRANCISCO SHOCKWAVES

Ryker ~ Aiden ~ Tristan

Damien ~ Blake

AUSTIN FUSION

Zack

ACKNOWLEDGMENTS

H, J & E - Thank you for encouraging me to write all these stories that keep me up at night. Thank you for all the time you give me to hide away and type all the words!

Tessa - Thanks for the inspiration for Raven's best friend! She was a fun character to write!

Renee - I seriously couldn't do this without you! It is crazy sometimes how alike we think!

Crystal - Thank you for joining my team when I was in a bind! You were the voice of reason when I needed it the most.

Dani - Thank you for always being there when I need someone to bounce an idea off or to calm my nerves because of something that is just a tiny issue but feels like a mountain in that moment.

My readers! You are the real MVPs here! Thank you for reading my books and loving my characters as much as I do.

xoxo,

Samantha

ABOUT THE AUTHOR

Samantha Lind is a *USA TODAY* Bestselling contemporary romance author. When she's not dreaming up new stories, she can often be found with her family, traveling, reading, watching her boys on the ice or watching her favorite professional team (Go Knights Go!).

Connect with Samantha in the following places:
www.samanthalind.com
samantha@samanthalind.com

Reader Group
Samantha Lind's Alpha Loving Ladies
Good Reads
https://goo.gl/t3R9Vm
Newsletter
https://bit.ly/FDSLNL

facebook.com/SamanthaLindAuthor
x.com/samanthalind1
instagram.com/samanthalindauthor
bookbub.com/authors/samantha-lind

www.ingramcontent.com/pod-product-compliance
Lightning Source LLC
Chambersburg PA
CBHW061810190726

48289CB00007B/2138